RV is a good kid, starting his freshman year at the demanding Boston Latin School. Though his genes didn't give him a lot of good things, they did give him a decent brain. So he's doing his best to keep up in high school, despite all the additional pressures he's facing: His immigrant parents, who don't want him to forget his roots and insist on other rules. Some tough kids at school who bully teachers as well as students. His puny muscles. His mean gym teacher. The Guy Upstairs who doesn't answer his prayers. And the most confusing fact of all—that he might be gay.

Luckily, RV develops a friendship with Mr. Aniso, his Latin teacher, who is gay and always there to talk to. RV thinks his problems are solved when he starts going out with Carole. But things only get more complicated when RV develops a crush on Bobby, the football player in his class. And to RV's surprise, Bobby admits he may have gay feelings, too.

Why Can't Life Be Like Pizza?

The Pizza Chronicles, Book One

Andy V. Roamer

A NineStar Press Publication

Published by NineStar Press
P.O. Box 91792,
Albuquerque, New Mexico, 87199 USA.
www.ninestarpress.com

Why Can't Life Be Like Pizza?

Printed in the USA
First Edition
March, 2020

Print ISBN: 978-1-951880-67-5

Also available in eBook, ISBN: 978-1-951880-66-8

Warning: This book contains homophobic bullying, homophobic slurs, physical abuse, mentions of gay bashing, racism within a character's family.

For Mom, who reminded me that you have to have guts to accomplish anything in this world—and shows me how to do it every day.

Chapter One

Why Can't Life Be Like Pizza?

Why can't life be like pizza?

I've been asking myself the question a lot lately. I love pizza. Pizza makes me feel good. Especially since I discovered Joe's. Joe's Pizza is quiet and out of the way and allows me to think. And Joe's combinations are the best. Pepperoni and onions. Garlic and mushroom. Cheese and chicken. And if you really want that little kick in the old butt: the super jalapeno. Mmmm, good. Gets you going again. And lets you forget all your troubles.

What troubles can a fourteen-year-old guy have? Ha! First of all, I'm not a regular guy, as anyone can guess from my taste in pizza. My parents are immigrants who are trying to make a better life for themselves here in the United States. Besides the usual things American parents worry about, like making money and having their kids do well in school, my parents spend more time worrying about the big things: politics, communism, fascism, global terror, and the fact they and their parents survived violence and jail so I-better-be-grateful-I'm-not-miserable-like-kids-in-other-parts-of-the-world.

Grateful? Ha! As far as I'm concerned, life is pretty miserable already. Instead of thinking about the World Series or Disneyland, I worry about terrorists down the street or the dirty bombs the strange family around the corner might be building.

I don't know why I worry about everything, but I do. It's probably in my genes. Other guys have genes that gave them big muscles or hairy chests. I got nerves.

And then there's my name. RV. Yeah, RV. No, I'm not a camper or anything. RV is short for Arvydas. That's right. "Are-vee-duh-s." Mom and Dad say it's a common name in Lithuania, which is the country in Eastern Europe where my parents were born. A name like that might be fine for Lithuania, but what about the United States? Couldn't Mom and Dad have named me Joe, or Mike, or even Darryl? My brother, Ray, has a normal name. Why couldn't they have given me one?

I even look a little weird, I think. Tall and skinny with an uncoordinated walk because of my big feet that get in the way and make me feel like a clod. Oh, yeah. I've been getting some zits lately, and I wear glasses since I'm pretty nearsighted. Not a pretty sight, is it? At least the glasses are not too thick. Mom and Dad don't have a lot of money to spend, but they did fork up the money to get me thin lenses, so I don't look like a complete zomboid.

What can I do? I try my best, despite it all. I'm lucky because I've done well in school, so at least my genes gave me a half-decent brain. Hey, I'm not bragging. It's just nice to feel good about something when most days I feel pretty much a loser at so many things. When I was in grammar school, there were enough days when I came home from school and cried because some big oaf threatened me, or I got hit in the stomach during my pathetic attempts to play ball during recess.

Mom always tried to comfort me. "*Nesirūpink,*" she would say. "*Esi gabus. Kai užaugsi, visiems nušluostysi nuosis.*" We talk Lithuanian at home. Translated, that sentence means, "Don't worry. You're smart. When you grow up, you'll show them." Actually, not "you'll show them," but "you'll wipe all their noses." Lithuanians have a funny way of expressing themselves. Not sure I aspire to wiping anyone's nose when I get older, but that's what they say.

Whatever. I'm determined to put all that behind me. I'm starting a new life. My new life. Today was the first day of high school. I'm going to Boston Latin School. You have to take an exam to go there, so it's full of smart kids. Besides smart kids, it has heavy-duty history too. It was founded in 1635, a year before Harvard. They already gave us a speech about that.

And about pressure. The pressure to succeed with all this history breathing down our necks. Pressure, ha! Doesn't scare me. I know all about pressure. I've gotten pressure from cretinous bullies at school. I get it from cretinous Lith a-holes, who Mom and Dad keep pushing me to hang around with because they say it's important to be part of the immigrant community. And I even get pressure from cretinous jerks in the neighborhood.

Cretinous. A good word. That's something else about me. I like words. Real words and made-up ones. There's something cool about them. Yeah, yeah, I know what people would say. You think words are cool? Kid, you've got more problems than you thought.

Well, I'm sorry. I do think words are cool. There's something fun about making them up or learning a new one. Kind of unlocks something in the world. And I like the world despite all my worrying. It can be an okay place sometimes.

Okay, okay, I'm getting off track. I want to write about my first day of school. Mom and Dad gave me this new— well, refurbished, but new to me anyway—computer for getting into Latin school, and they keep after me to make good use of it. So, I've decided I'm going to write about my new life. My life away from cretins—Lith, American, or any other kind.

The first person I met at school today was Carole. Carole Higginbottom. She's in my homeroom. She was sitting in the first row, first seat, and I was sitting right behind her. We started talking. She's from West Roxbury, too, which is where we live.

West Roxbury is part of Boston. You have to live somewhere in Boston in order to go to Latin school. West Roxbury is a nice neighborhood, for the most part, with houses, trees, grass, and people going to work and coming home. Kind of an all-American place, I guess. We used to live in a different, tougher part of Boston, but Mom and Dad moved away from there because they said the neighborhood was getting too rough. They promised I wouldn't get beat up so much in West Roxbury. I don't know. West Roxbury is better, but I still have gotten a few black-and-blue marks with "made in West Roxbury" on them, so as far as I'm concerned it isn't any perfect place either.

Carole lives in another part of West Roxbury, near Centre Street, which is the main street in the area. People like to hang out there. Mom says that part of West Roxbury is a little dicey. (Mom thinks a lot of neighborhoods are too dicey. Maybe that's where I get my worrying from.) Anyway, Carole sure doesn't seem dicey. As a matter of fact, she's a little goofy. Tall and skinny with red hair, red cheeks, and a million freckles. And she has a really sharp nose that curves up like those special ski slopes you see in the Olympics. But I get the feeling she's smart. She says she likes science. That's good because I might need help with science. I'm better with other subjects like history and English.

Our homeroom teacher is Mr. Bologna, Carmine Bologna. He's a little scary with slicked-back dark hair and even darker eyes that stare at you forever. He looks like he's part of the organization we're not supposed to talk about—you know, the scary one from Italy that's into murder, racketeering, and drugs. Two guys were horsing around in the back of the class and Mr. Bologna came right up to them, said a few words under his breath, and just stared at them. Boy, did they settle down fast. I'm no troublemaker, but I'll really have to watch myself. Don't want to deal with the Bologna stare if I can help it.

Today was mostly about walking around, learning about our subjects, and meeting teachers. Besides all the regular subjects, I have to take Latin. I don't have anything against it per se, but is it really necessary to learn a dead language? And then there's the teacher, Mr. Aniso. He's kind of light in his loafers. That's another new phrase I learned recently. It refers to gay guys, and Mr. Aniso is so gay it hurts. I just hope he can't tell anything about me. I don't wave my wrist around the way he does, do I?

Yeah, that's something else I have to come to terms with. I might be heading in that direction. Yeah, me. I can hardly believe it. Me! Why? It can't be true, can it? I've been praying to God, asking Him not to make me gay, but I don't think He's listening. If He exists, that is. Maybe He's not answering because He doesn't exist.

I don't know. People on TV and in books say being gay is okay. Movie stars and rock stars are gay. There are gay mayors and other gay political types. That's fine for them, but they don't live with my family. Mom's a heavy-duty Catholic. Dad's a macho, "what-me-cry?" kind of guy. And my younger brother, Ray, well, Ray probably doesn't care one way or another, but he doesn't count anyway since he hates everybody. And then there are all those Lith immigrants, the community that's so important to Mom and Dad. Most of them are so Old World and conservative. I don't think being gay would go down well with them.

Not that I am gay for certain. I'm just saying it's crossed my mind because...well, because I think about guys sometimes. And I notice them. Notice how they look when they're coming down the street. Notice their eyes or their hair or the way they move. Just notice them.

Oh, I notice girls, too, but something about guys is different. I can't put my finger on it, but I think about them as much or maybe more than girls. And I want to be with them. Is that normal? What's normal anyway? To be honest, I'm so inexperienced. Never dated. Never even kissed anyone. Not like *that* anyway. No, I've spent my time worrying about communism, terrorism, and global terror. Like I said, I've always felt a little out of step with the rest of humanity.

Dealing with all this is just too much. To be nervous about things the way I am. To be speaking a language most people haven't heard of. To have a strange name. To wear glasses and look nerdy. And now I might be gay? It's all too confusing. I might as well start on antidepressants, or something stronger, right now.

But no. I try to look on the bright side of things. Take Carole for instance. She seems nice and fun, and maybe we'll be friends. And if she likes me, I can't be too weird, can I? I guess I'll find out. I better not think about it. There's enough to worry about as it is. I just have to take a breath and focus on my homework. Yeah, we got homework already. At least that's one thing I'm good at. And when I go to Joe's, well, life's not so bad, at least while I'm eating my chicken and cheese or super jalapeno slice.

Chapter Two

What's My Heritage?

Being a Lith is a big part of my life. Excuse me, being of Lithuanian extraction, as some of my parents' friends call it. Lithuanian extraction. Sounds like some weird creature plucked out of a test tube, doesn't it? Anyway, being of Lithuanian extraction, I had to go to Lith school on Saturdays until last spring when I finished eighth grade. Every Saturday for eight years, except during summers. That's a big chunk of my life.

Makes you think about how precious life is. And you don't want to waste any of it.

Maybe that's why Ray is so bent out of shape so often. He still goes to Litsky School, as we call it. He probably thinks he's wasting his life even more than I did. And now that I don't have to go anymore he's jealous.

Well, too bad. I put in my time, and he has to also. Part of the duties of being a kid of immigrants, I suppose. Besides, it's not like I don't have to do other Lith stuff. The whole family often goes to Lith church on Sundays. As I said, Mom's really into being the good Catholic, and she tries to make sure we're good Catholics too. She makes sure we all go to church, practically every Sunday, and she even sings in the choir to show how committed she is.

There are a whole bunch of other Lith events: picnics, parties, dances, lectures, and visitors from the Old Country who give talks and perform. That's fine. Some of these things aren't so bad. But some of them are for the birds. And they usually happen on Sundays. A great way to spend half your weekend.

Whenever Ray and I grumble and ask why we have to go to yet another Lith event, Mom and Dad always say one thing. "*Čia jūsų paveldas.*" "Because it's your heritage."

Heritage. If I've heard the word once I've heard it a thousand times. Heritage. Heritage. Heritage. What does it mean? The dictionary says it's your inheritance, your birthright. Mom and Dad use the word as an excuse for a lot of things. They don't want us to talk English in the house. They want us to have more Lith friends. They make us go to Lith school and Lith church. They feed us strange Lith food. Where is it all going to end?

I understand history and its importance. Mom and Dad came to the US when they were still pretty young. I know things weren't easy for them. Lithuania had been part of the Soviet Union but declared independence in 1990. Mom and Dad's parents marched and even went to jail, agitating for freedom. Mom and Dad felt lucky to grow up in a free country, but life was hard after independence. Mom and Dad tell me the capitalists who took over the country were almost as bad as the communists who had run it before. They didn't know each other then, but Mom left her family, and Dad left his family, and they both moved to America for a better life. (Mom and Dad have since learned the US is run by capitalists too. But they say American capitalists are better than Lithuanian ones, though not by much.)

Mom and Dad met here in the States. I once asked them why they got married. They looked at each other as if they didn't know what to say. I know they went through a lot to come here and make a life. Maybe that's their bond.

Trouble is, after everything, I'm not sure Mom and Dad are so happy to be here in the US. They complain about this country constantly. Especially Dad. This thing isn't good in the US or that thing was better in the Old Country. If he's not happy here I'm sorry. What am I supposed to do about it? Am I stuck with his heritage? I have my hands full managing my own life. I have my own heritage, don't I?

If you tell Mom and Dad you want a life of your own, that maybe you don't want to go to some stupid event, they don't like to hear it.

"Look at the So-and-Sos," they tell us. "Their kids aren't sitting at home in front of the TV." Except of course they say it in the mother tongue, since talking English at home is forbidden. Another symptom of losing your heritage. So we hear about the model families with kids who get good marks in Lith School and are active in a bunch of Lith organizations. Super Liths, I call them. Mom and Dad, especially Dad, want us to be Super Liths too. Too bad if we're just regular Liths. Sure, we watch TV. But no more than the average all-American kid.

But Mom and Dad always seem to be afraid we're turning into regular Americans. What's wrong with that? I don't know why, but the idea scares them. They keep repeating we're of Lithuanian extraction, so we're *Lithuanian*-Americans.

With an emphasis on Lithuanian.

"We were born here," my brother likes to remind them, speaking in English.

"If you born in barn, you horse?" Dad replies in one of his woeful attempts at English.

You just can't win. So, we go to all those events. And keep our mouths shut. At least I do even if Ray keeps grumbling.

Mom understands our frustration a little more than Dad. Even though being a Lith is important to her, I think she likes being an American too. She has a lot of American friends and goes to movies and shows with them when she can. Dad doesn't do any of that. I don't think he has any friends who aren't from the Old Country. If he wants to have fun, he goes to the Lith Club.

Ah, the Lith Club. How often have we been dragged there? The club is in South Boston, which is where a lot of Liths settled when they arrived in Boston a long time ago. It's an all-purpose club. Upstairs is a hall where we hear concerts, see plays, and listen to boring speeches about Lith politics and history. Downstairs in the basement is a pizza joint. The cool people escape there and have some of the delicious Lith food they serve besides pizza like potato dumplings with sour cream and bacon. Or soup made from beets with more sour cream. Really good for your arteries. The pizza is about the healthiest thing there.

On the ground floor is a bar, which is really good for your liver. Dad goes there. It's his escape. He says it's a good place to get away from life's daily troubles and relax with his friends. I guess these guys feel they went through a lot escaping the communists and bad capitalists in the Old Country. So now they need to escape problems here in this country. But sometimes they seem to spend more time escaping than doing anything else.

Today we had to go to the Lith Club because a chorus from the Old Country was performing. Mom's a singer from way back, so she loves going to these concerts. Like I said, she even sings in church on Sundays. Ray escaped the concert as he usually does, disappearing somewhere, probably hanging out with his cool friends at the pizza joint downstairs. I'm not a cool kid, so I stayed upstairs as

I usually do. Sometimes I can sneak to the back, find a quiet corner, and read a book. Sometimes I'm actually interested in what's going on. And sometimes I have to hang out with my cousins, the Shalinskai.

Their name is pronounced "Sh-ahh-linss-kai." I call them the S-heads, ha ha. They're Mom's relatives who live in Wellesley, a ritzy suburb of Boston. We don't see them much, which is fine by me. They're Super Liths, too, but snooty in a polite kind of way, which makes them even harder to take. They have two kids: Jonas, who's sixteen, and Jolanda, who's thirteen. Jonas already knows he's going to be a doctor like his father, who's a surgeon. And Jolanda is going to be a model because she's so beautiful.

Mom's not even sure how they're related. Some distant cousin supposedly fell in love with another distant cousin in the Old Country. But I think there's more to the whole story. From what I know of history in that part of the world, it's likely some Cossack raped a farm girl before bringing her back to meet his folks. That's how they did things in those days.

The S-heads were at the concert today. Jonas and Jolanda were even part of the program, giving a welcome greeting to the singers. Jolanda recited a poem she wrote. I might not know my way around poetry, but I do know my way around BS, that's for sure.

After he finished with his part of the program, Jonas came up to me at the back of the hall where I was quietly reading my book. "Hey, RV. So how's life at Latin school?" he asked.

"Okay," I said, shrugging. I didn't want to go into any details. Jonas goes to some fancy prep school, and his mother keeps bragging how great his grades are.

He looked at the book in my hands. "What are you reading?"

I showed him the book, *Heart of Darkness*. "I'm reading it for school."

"Oh! The horror! The horror!" Jonas said, making a face. "Isn't that what the guy says at the end?"

"I don't know. I haven't gotten to the end yet. But thanks for telling me."

"Oh, sorry, RV," Jonas didn't seem concerned. "Don't worry, not much happens. Just say it's about man's inhumanity to man and how western countries exploited Africa, and you'll get an A for your book report."

Jonas can be a real snot. I thought of the unlucky people who would be Jonas's patients. "Oh, you have cancer? So sorry, dude. Go get some radiation and call me in the morning."

I was trying to think of an excuse to escape Jonas when he suggested I go downstairs with him and his friends.

I started to shake my head but Jonas insisted. "Come on, RV," he said. "We don't spend enough time together. You don't want to listen to these boring singers, do you?"

He was right on that point. I wasn't much into music anyway, and certainly didn't care about singers from six thousand miles away.

So I agreed.

B-a-a-d move! We went downstairs to the pizza joint. I didn't see Ray, who wouldn't have wanted to hang out with me anyway. I had a pizza with Jonas and some of his friends, which was fine. When he's not being snooty, Jonas can be fun, and I was starting to have a good time.

But then everyone went out back somewhere behind the bar. Jonas took out some cigarettes and a bottle of some kind and passed everything around. I tried to say no at first, but that didn't go over too well. "Oh, come on, RV." "We won't tell anyone, RV." "You're in high school now, RV."

So I joined them. I don't know how much I smoked or how many drinks I had, but by the time I went back upstairs, I was feeling pretty lousy. The singers had stopped singing, and my parents were now sitting around big tables with the S-heads and other friends, eating and drinking and having a good time, which they often do after these events. Just the smell of food about did me in, though, and before I could make it to the bathroom, I threw up all over the floor.

Needless to say, Mom and Dad weren't pleased. I told them I wasn't feeling well, which was true. They looked a little suspicious, but they didn't give me a hard time. They said it was time to go home and found my brother, who reappeared from somewhere. Who knows what he was doing, but he looked fine. How come he can get away with God knows what, and I can't?

As we walked out of the hall I passed by Jonas.

He gave me a fake look of concern "RV. Are you okay?"

"Yeah, I'm fine."

Another person who can get away with God knows what, I thought. Everyone can get away with things except me.

*

I'm sitting here trying to do some homework, but I can't concentrate. I'm still thinking about the stupid concert. Why did I let Jonas talk me into going downstairs? What was I trying to prove?

Sometimes I feel like I'm made of different parts and I can't figure out how they all fit together anymore. At the beginning of my life, the Lith stuff was the most important. If I left it to Mom and Dad, it still would be. But they'll have to accept I'm starting a new life and maybe things are changing. The Lith stuff is part of me, but there are a lot of other parts too. More important parts.

It's good to sit here in front of the computer and let out everything I keep bottled up. When I do, I usually feel better. Maybe I can catch up on some homework now. Even though it's only the start of the school year, we already have a ton of work to do. I can see a lot of kids at Latin school are even smarter than I thought. You have to work hard to keep up with everybody. At least I know I can work hard. Maybe that's my heritage.

Chapter Three

Mesmerized

Amo. Amas. Amat.

Amo. Amas. Amat.

I love. You love. He or she loves.

That was us in Mr. Aniso's class today. Over and over again. Conjugating "to love" in Latin.

We don't have verb conjugation in English, so some of the kids find the concept hard to wrap their minds around. Lithuanian works the same way, so I get it. And I don't hate that part.

What I do hate is Mr. Aniso's way of teaching. He's so big on repetition. He was walking up and down the aisles, making all of us repeat the words over and over again. Like little robots.

If only Mr. Aniso knew what the kids were doing behind his back, maybe he'd stop walking past them. Everyone makes faces and hand gestures you wouldn't want to wish on your worst enemy. I suppose Mr. Aniso is partly to blame. Why does he swish so much? And his wrists are so limp they make spaghetti look tough by comparison.

If I turn out like that I'm going to kill myself. Really. I can't go through life like Mr. Aniso. His voice is another problem. He usually talks very softly, like a woman reading poetry. But when he gets irritated, his voice gets really high and screechy, and you just want to cover your ears and run out of the room.

I can't be gay. I can't be! Bi, maybe, but not gay. Not if I'm going to sound like Mr. Aniso. I've been listening to my voice and I think it's getting a little too high for my own good. I'm going to buy a recorder and listen to myself talking out loud every night. Maybe I'll even read a few pages from a book. I think there's a way to make your voice deeper by moving the sounds you make to the back of your throat. I've got to practice the technique. Words come out a little scratchy, but at least they don't sound like a woman reading poetry.

I've been watching my hand and body movements too. Not the most masculine, I have to admit. Like the way I raise my hand in class. I hate the way I raise my hand! Why didn't I ever notice it before? My arm goes up slowly and kind of hangs there, like a wilted flower. It should shoot straight up, fast, like a rocket. And stay there—no wilting allowed. And when I put it down, it should go back down with determination, not float down the way it does now, so namby-pamby like.

Sometimes I think no matter how hard I try to change things, the gay part of me is getting stronger and stronger. Like when I watch the jocks practice. There's a ball field near our house with some woods behind it. Teams from various schools practice there. I've found a nice spot at the edge of the field, under a tree. I started going there earlier this summer to think or to read a book. But lately, I've put the book down and have started watching football players practicing. It's more intense than when I notice guys on the street. I see more things. The way they move so fast. The way they catch and throw the football so effortlessly. The way they pat one another on the backs or butts all the time. Everything looks so free and easy. I want to be like them. I want to be with them.

Yeah. I realize I'm not just watching anymore. I'm mesmerized. I can't look away, no matter how hard I try. Mesmerized is another good word I learned, and I think it's pretty accurate in describing what's going on. When you're mesmerized, it's like you don't have any power over the thing that has your attention. I try to look away sometimes, but I just can't.

I've been praying about what's happening to me. Yeah. I said I wasn't sure about God. But I haven't given up. Just in case. So I pray. "O God, why am I so interested in watching these guys? Am I as interested in watching girls on the beach? Am I heading in a gay direction? Please. Give me a sign."

I haven't gotten a sign yet. So, I throw in other people too—Jesus, John the Baptist, some of the prophets, even the Virgin Mary. "If the Big Guy is too busy, maybe you guys can hear me. I'm having a hard time these days. Am I really going to be gay? I don't think I can deal with that. Maybe bi, but not now. Not with everything else going on in my life. It's hard enough as it is right now. So, you guys have got to help and change how things are going. Please."

I thought maybe someone up there was listening when I found a new copy of one of those girlie magazines a few weeks ago. I can't look at naked women on the internet because Mom and Dad monitor the websites I go to. That was our agreement for their getting me my own computer. My diary is private and password protected, but they have a right to check the websites I visit on the computer and my phone. I can live with that—for now.

But finding the girlie magazine was like a gift from one of those guys I've been praying to. It was outside our supermarket, so someone must have dropped it when they were taking their groceries to the car. One man's trash is another man's treasure! I scooped it up and brought it home before anyone could see me.

I've been looking at all the naked women in it, ever since. It's one of those special retrospective issues, and my favorites are Miss January and Miss July. These women are pretty and sexy all right. And I enjoy looking at them. But then I think about the jocks on the field again, and I forget about Miss January and Miss July. So fast. Thinking about the guys on the field is just, I don't know, more exciting. So that's a sign I'm heading in the gay direction, right?

Can it be true? Can it really be true? I'm one of *them?* In grammar school, which was Catholic of course, they brought in Father Flynn to talk about sexuality. He seemed like a good guy, but in the end he had to stick with the Church's position that falling in love with someone of the opposite sex and having children is what it's all about. The ideal, according to Father Flynn.

Someone did ask him about other forms of sexuality, and he did agree that "we can't always live up to our ideals," adding that life isn't perfect.

Life isn't perfect? Hello! I could have told you that the minute I came out of the womb. I strive for the ideal too. But this sex stuff has me flummoxed. Flummoxed. Another good word. Sounds like how I feel most days. Confused and all over the place. If I ever write my autobiography, maybe that's what I should call it. *My Life Being Flummoxed*, by RV. Ha, ha.

But I don't want to be flummoxed. Not for my whole life. Is that why I haven't given up praying? Something else I took away from my first eight years at Catholic school? They kept telling us you have to have faith. So, I guess I have faith. And I keep hoping things will get clear to me someday.

Meanwhile, I'll try not to get too worked up about my life. One has to keep going, right? Maybe everyone up there doesn't answer me because they're just too busy answering other people. I know a lot of people have problems in this world, so maybe it's just a long waiting line, and we all have to take a number. Whether it's true or not, believing this makes me feel better. So, I'm waiting. I just hope I'll get to the head of the line sooner rather than later.

Chapter Four

New Ventures with Carole

I've been hanging out with Carole Higginbottom more and more. She's even goofier than I thought when I first met her, and she says off-the-wall things sometimes. But I like her. And she seems to like me. Her father is in the army and they move around a lot. Carole seems kind of lonely, maybe because she's never been in a place long enough to learn how to make friends. And maybe that's why she likes me. She doesn't know any better.

There I go, putting myself down again. No, maybe Carole likes me because...because she likes me. I help her with Spanish and English (her spelling is terrible!), and she helps me with math. She's really a whiz at math. We're doing algebra in math class and I usually get what Mr. Dusenberg, our math teacher, is talking about—after one or two tries. It just takes my brain time to process all that stuff. But Carole? Mr. Dusenberg only has to put an equation on the board and she's already raising her hand either answering a question or asking something really complicated. I wish I could glimpse into her brain sometimes. I wonder if I'd see equations floating around in there.

Carole and I have started getting together after school when we have free time. We're hatching a scheme. A business scheme. (Hatching a scheme. It's such a neat phrase. Makes me feel like I'm doing something secret. Which is kind of exciting.)

Carole and I are going into the fix-it business. Not just any fix-it business, but a fix-it business for computers and other electronic stuff. Carole is really good with these things, and we figure there are a lot of people who could use some help with their equipment. I'm not exactly sure what I bring to the table, but Carole says I'm really organized so I can be the bookkeeper and money person. I guess my math is good enough for that. Carole said I'm the CFO—Chief Financial Officer. I guess that would make her the CEO.

We put up signs around the neighborhood and online, and already got our first client: Mr. O'Malley. He lives a few houses down from me. He's a widower. His wife died a few years ago, and he's been a real sourpuss ever since. He's always yelling at kids to get off his property. He never smiles when you say good morning. And in general, he's the kind of person you avoid whenever you can.

So I was surprised when he called me the other day. Our first job! We're going over to his house tomorrow after school. He got a new computer and he needs help setting it up. I'm a little nervous since it's Mr. O'Malley. I hope he doesn't give us a hard time or refuse to pay us for the work or something. Carole made me call him back and tell him we wanted half the payment up front. "It's the way real businesses work," she said. "Down payments."

Mr. O'Malley did get mad when I told him we wanted a down payment. I thought he was going to hang up but then he must have thought better of it because he offered to give us a third of the money up front. I agreed to that.

"Good," Carole said when I told her. "Real businesses have to negotiate prices too."

Whew! Passed my first test. We'll be a great team.

*

I don't know where to begin. I'm so confused and all over the place, I can hardly write. Okay. Okay. I better take a breath and say what happened at Mr. O'Malley's house. It will give me a chance to think things through.

Mr. O'Malley didn't yell at us or refuse to pay or anything like that. He was still a sourpuss, but I think he's happy with the work we did. We hooked up the computer, and it works fine. Mr. O'Malley paid us like we had agreed. He even offered us some ginger ale when we were done.

No. My all-over-the-place feeling has nothing to do with Mr. O'Malley. It has to do with Carole.

The computer terminal was on a desk near the wall. To hook it up to the printer Carole had to squeeze behind the desk. But she couldn't reach some wires, so she asked me to squeeze in beside her and grab one that was really hard to get. So, I did. I had to lean over really far in order to reach the wire, and I found myself practically on top of Carole. I couldn't turn my head and see her face, but her breath was on my ear. It felt funny but good.

Then I tried to hand the wire to Carole. But when I did, I kind of squeezed both of us into the tiny space even more. I could hardly breathe. Carole was still breathing though. Her breath was on my cheek now, and her lips were brushing against my cheek. Almost as though she was trying to kiss me. Her body felt warm against mine.

I wanted to stay in that position a little longer, but Carole moved this way and another way and wriggled out from under me.

"Whew, that was a tight squeeze," she said with a strange smile. I think she was blushing a little bit. Since she's a redhead, she blushes pretty easily—almost as much as me. Maybe that's the real reason she likes me—she's met someone who blushes more than she does.

Anyway, I was just kind of lying there like a jerk, panting, not knowing what to say. Carole went back to hooking up the computer pretty quickly, while I kept lying there in a daze, thinking about me lying on top of her, squeezed so closely together.

I'm still thinking about it. Maybe someone up there has finally started listening to me. I liked Carole's warm body against mine. I wonder what would happen if we were doing something else, like necking?

I'm promising myself this afternoon not to go to the ball field or watch the jocks. No matter how good they look. I'm going to think of Carole without her clothes on. She's pretty skinny, and her body is nothing like Miss January's or Miss July's. But life's not perfect as I've already learned. Carole's body against mine was real, and it felt good, and maybe I'm not so gay after all.

Now I can't wait for tonight! I'm feeling good about life again. I have a lot of homework to do, so I hope I can concentrate long enough to get it out of the way before I shut the lights and start thinking about Carole and me in that tight squeeze. And her breath on my ear. And her body close to mine.

*

So much for feeling positive about life. It's almost midnight, but I need to write this down. I tried to think about Carole as I went to bed. I tried really hard. I thought about what she might look like coming into my room without clothes. I even tried putting her face on Miss January's body and imagining her standing in front of my bed doing a sexy dance.

It only worked up to a point. In the beginning, Carole was in my mind doing all those sexy poses. And she looked great. But she disappeared after a little while. I had to keep trying to bring her back into my thoughts. But then some of the jocks appeared. Without my trying too hard. I did my best to get rid of them, but it wasn't easy. Especially when I remembered how they looked when they took their shirts off. They were there, big and clear in my mind. It was tough for Carole to compete, even with the help of Miss January's body.

I told myself maybe I didn't do things right. Maybe I should have concentrated better. Or maybe if I spend more time with Carole it will be easier to keep her sexy poses in my thoughts. That's it, I decided. I'll spend more time with her. Maybe I'll just grab her and kiss her and even feel her up a little.

And then I just about lost it, when I realized I didn't even finish my algebra homework. That got me upset too. Trying to figure out all these things is taking over my life. If I don't watch it, school will suffer, and then I'll really be in trouble. Luckily, I fell asleep and was able to put everything out of my mind. Except the memories of the guys on the field, running and jumping and patting one another on their butts.

Chapter Five

Frozen Moments

Mom and Dad had an argument. A big one. They argue a lot. Sometimes about important things, sometimes about stupid things. Often, it's about money.

Today's fight started at dinner where they usually start. It's ironic—another good word. It means things should be one way but they turn out the opposite. Kind of like the whole world works, I suppose. A good thing to remember.

Anyway, dinners are the one time when the family is all together. Having everybody together for dinner is a big deal for Dad. He insists on it. "*Šeima yra viskas*," he says. "Family is everything." After "it's your heritage," "the family" is the thing we hear second most often around the house.

Maybe family is important to Dad because he was so close to the people he left behind to come to the US. His three sisters besides his parents. And he's still close to them. Emails them and talks to them on the phone. Mom didn't have any brothers or sisters. And from what she's told us, she wasn't that close to her parents, since they were always marching and working for independence. She was left with a grandmother, who ended up dying. So I imagine who you left behind in the Old Country influences how you feel about it compared to the US.

Today at dinner, Mom and Dad were talking about nothing in particular, when Dad mentioned he had to go to the post office to mail a package. He had bought some stuff to send to his sisters and their families back home.

Mom made a face and asked him what he was sending.

He looked a little guilty and said just some presents and other things.

Mom asked for more details but he wouldn't tell her.

That's a sore point for Mom. She's often asking Dad for more money to get things, sometimes for the house, sometimes for me and Ray or herself, but he resists, telling her to be more careful with the money she has. She then points out to him if he didn't send so much to the Old Country, he'd have more money to spend here.

And that's what happened today. Mom reminded him he had just sent a big care package to his sisters a month before.

He got mad and told her she was being selfish, that he was doing it for his family.

She told him he had a family here too.

Ray and I were just happy to finish our meals, leave the table, and go to our rooms upstairs. But Mom and Dad continued arguing. They both started yelling louder and louder. A dish banged against a table, and there was some more yelling. Then a door slammed, and finally everything was quiet.

I wanted to go downstairs to see if everything was okay, but I just sat at my desk, frozen, afraid to breathe. It's not the first time they've had such a huge fight. These arguments really get to me. Dad's a big, muscular guy and pretty intimidating. I guess he has to be since he's a foreman at a construction company and has to supervise all those other construction workers. But when he gets angry, he's scary. His dark eyes become even darker, and he stares right through you. His muscles tense up like he's about to explode.

I'm afraid he'll hit Mom sometimes, which he has done a couple of times. The last time Mom said this was it; if he did it again, she would leave him. Thank God that hasn't happened. But I worry. When they argue, they really get into it, and I'm afraid Dad might lose it sometime. I also wish Mom would back off when he gets really upset, but she doesn't. I guess she feels she has every right to stand up to him, which she says is the American way. Not that Dad agrees, of course. I just wish I didn't worry about it so much. I even tell myself that since I'm older now I should be able to do something to stop the arguments. But what? It's not my job, is it?

But what is my job? Not to sit in my room at my desk, unable to move. I'm afraid to breathe, afraid to do anything, waiting for everything to calm down. I hate that about myself. Wanting to do something, but unable to. Stuck in a frozen moment, feeling so inadequate.

I just couldn't sit there any longer today. I tiptoed over to my brother's room. His room is upstairs, too, across from mine. Ray's way of drowning out the fighting is to put on his headphones and listen to music—turning it up as loud as he can. It's so loud I can hear the music from my room sometimes. It pisses me off because I like things quiet. But Ray, well, we all have our ways of coping, I suppose.

I went up to Ray's door and knocked. I had to knock and shake the door hard a couple of times before he heard me.

"You heard all that yelling and banging?" I asked when he finally opened the door. "Do you think everything's all right?"

He shrugged. "Yeah, probably. They're not fighting now." He didn't seem too upset about it. He was probably more upset that I had disturbed him. He just stood there by the door, looking at me. *So what do you want me to do about it, RV?* I'm sure that's what he was thinking. Then, he turned around, went back to his bed, and put his headphones back on.

I stood in the doorway, trying to figure out what to do. Ray was already lost in the music, lying on his bed with his eyes closed, thumping his fingers to the beat of whatever song he was listening to. It was clear he wasn't interested in continuing any conversation with me.

I was annoyed, but I've long since stopped trying to get Ray to help me solve our family problems. As a matter of fact, he is one of the problems. He does his share of arguing with Dad. And he argues with Mom too. No matter what they say, he either disappears somewhere for hours, or if he is home, he goes to his room, shuts the door, and listens to his music.

And he doesn't seem afraid of Dad—at least until Dad really loses it. When that happens, Dad hits Ray, sometimes pretty hard. Then Mom starts yelling and tries to intervene, telling both of them to stop. When things finally let up, Ray just runs out of the house or goes up to his room.

And what do I do? I stand there unable to move, afraid to do anything. My frozen moments. There are a lot of them, and I'm not proud of them. But I can't stop them. My only other option is to run up to my room and hide.

Ray's never said anything to me about my frozen moments, but I wonder if he resents me for not standing up to Dad more. I'd like to ask him, but somehow I've never found the opportunity. I wish we were close, like real brothers, but we're more like strangers. Ray says "Good morning" to me and "What's on TV?" and things like that, but we don't have real conversations. I don't know his soul. And he certainly doesn't seem interested in mine.

I suddenly realized I was still standing in his doorway. And I got mad at myself for not knowing what to do. Another frozen RV moment. But I hate to think my parents are fighting. Or worrying things might get worse. And no matter how much I wish I could be like Ray, I just can't ignore their fights. I do care, and I want everything to be okay.

I finally made my decision, turned around, and went downstairs. Dad was sitting on the living room sofa, reading a paper. I could tell he was still angry. I wanted to pass by without talking to him, but he looked up from his paper.

When Dad stares up at you when he's upset, it's pretty intimidating. His big dark eyes hide something scary. Like something's about to explode behind them. And everything about Dad is big, including his muscles. Those muscles, especially his forearms, are huge, probably as big as my legs. I guess working in construction his muscles have to be developed. But he should thank his genes. Even if I lifted weights for a hundred years, I still wouldn't have arms half as big as Dad's.

Dad went on staring at me without saying anything. *"Kaip viskas?"* I said stupidly just to make conversation. "How are things?"

"*Matai, kaip.*" "You see how."

Dad was scowling, and he kept looking at me as if he wanted to say something else. But he kept quiet and finally looked back down at the paper.

I took the opportunity to get away from him. What more could I say? "Hey, Dad. Don't worry. Be happy?"

I went to Mom's room. Her door was closed, so I knocked as quietly as I could.

She told me to come in. She was sitting on her bed with a few pieces of jewelry spread out before her. Mom works part-time in the jewelry department of a big department store but keeps saying someday she wants to open her own jewelry store. I think she could too. She's very creative and has designed some jewelry for the store.

"*Ką dirbi?*" "What are you doing?" I asked.

She told me she was sorting through some of her jewelry for something at work. She looked back down at the bits and pieces on the bed, concentrating intensely on them. I knew that meant she was angry. She always tries to hide her anger by working hard. I asked her if everything was okay.

She finally looked up at me and nodded. "*O taip. Esu okay.*" "Oh, sure. I'm okay." Then she went back to her jewelry. Mom doesn't like to show she's upset. She likes to be strong. Or at least pretend she's strong. Is that good or bad? I don't know.

I kept quiet, not knowing what to say. Another RV Frozen Moment. Number two—or is it three?—in the last twenty minutes. Great night.

Ignoring me, Mom took a silver-colored necklace and put it next to a gold-colored one on the bed. "*Kuri tau gražesnė?*" she asked without looking up. "Which one do you think is prettier?" I mumbled something about both of them being pretty—like she was. I know she likes compliments, so I figured this was as good a time as any to pay her one.

Finally, she looked up at me and smiled. "*Ačiū*. Thank you." Then she shook her head. "*Nesirūpink, Arvydai. Viskas bus gerai.*" "Don't worry, RV. Everything will be all right." I wondered if she was trying to convince me or herself.

Mom went back to her jewelry, arranging the pieces in different ways on her bed. I wanted to ask her about her fight with Dad, reach out somehow. But I was afraid to say anything. I don't know why that is. Why we don't say what we really want to sometimes. If we did, would it make us feel better or worse?

Mom gave me another smile. "*Nesirūpink. Viskas bus gerai,*" she repeated. But she was back concentrating on the jewelry in a few seconds.

I turned around and left. I went back up to my room. Ray's door was closed again, though I could still hear the music blaring from his headphones. I tried to put my family out of my mind and do some homework. It gets me mad. School is important, and I have to figure out a way to do my work and not get caught up in my crazy family. I have to stop worrying about them and worry about myself. Maybe my brother is happy just listening to his music and shutting out the world. But not me. I want to be part of the world, enjoying it. Not feeling stuck in a frozen moment.

Chapter Six

Another New Venture with Carole

I've got to be braver with Carole. I'm such a wimp. I'm pretty sure she wouldn't mind getting a little romantic, but I haven't done anything much about it.

How do I know that? Well, I don't really know it, but I think so. She's been dropping enough hints. We saw a movie together last week. We've started to go to movies together. I love movies, and it turns out Carole does too. This was a love story. It was kind of mushy, but Carole liked it a lot. "I wonder how it feels to be so in love you can't think of anything else," she said as we were leaving the theatre.

"Yeah, I wonder," I said, though love isn't something I know too much about.

Then she gave me a funny look. "Wouldn't it be great to find out though," she said.

She's been giving me that look more and more lately. It's like a stare because she doesn't take her eyes off you. Her eyes are big and green, and they almost sparkle when she's gazing at you. Then she giggles and looks away like she feels guilty or embarrassed about something.

And dufus me, I just stare straight ahead and don't say anything like I didn't notice a thing.

Carole's also been coming up with some pretty strange kissy-face suggestions about things she wants us to try. She makes them up when we're with other people, so maybe they're not aimed at me, but I wonder. Like the other day, we were hanging out with a guy from school, Tim. Tim's a computer geek, and he said he'd help us with our fix-it business. (We've made $50 so far!) We were at Carole's house, and Tim showed her how to fix something on her computer. Then, when we were finished, we were all hanging out, drinking Cokes.

Carole said we should do something fun.

"Like what?" I asked.

"How about strip poker?" she suggested. And she had that funny look in her eyes again.

Tim's a pretty straitlaced, serious guy, and he laughed and shook his head. So, Carole said we could stop at our underwear. "I don't like anyone seeing my underwear," I told her.

So, then Carole suggested we play spin the bottle. That really made Tim nervous, so Carole added her own rules. She said you could pick a proxy, so if the bottle pointed to a person you didn't want to kiss, you could ask someone else to do the kissing. Of course, there were only the three of us, and she knew Tim and I wouldn't want to kiss each other. So, that would mean Carole would be kissing one of us with every spin of the stupid bottle. Needless to say, we didn't play that game either.

So, is Carole giving me hints or what? And what do I do about it? I liked those few seconds behind the desk at Mr. O'Malley's house, didn't I? And Carole didn't seem exactly displeased, did she? And now what's this with the strip poker and spin the bottle routine? If I wait too long she might give up on me and go for Tim. He's not one of the most handsome guys of this world, but I'm not either, am I?

*

I did it! I made a move, and Carole responded! Whoa! Whoa! I shouldn't get too ahead of myself. It was just a little step, kind of pathetic really, and I'm blushing when I write this. But it was something.

We did another computer job, helping a lady with her internet connection. It was a beautiful afternoon, so Carole suggested we take a walk through the woods that are adjacent to the ballpark in our neighborhood and then go get some pizza. I couldn't help wondering if she was giving me another hint.

We were both feeling good. Our business is going well, and we decided to take on Tim as a consultant. Carole really seems to have a head for business. She explained to Tim that we couldn't really afford another partner now, but she said we valued his work and could pay him on a per-job basis. Tim agreed, though I'm not so sure. He's so intense about anything electronic and gets frustrated when we don't understand one of his explanations. So, I'm wondering how long he'll put up with us. But Carole says it's a win-win for all of us. She's convinced Tim, so I'm going along with it.

Anyway, the walk through the woods was kind of romantic. It was a beautiful fall afternoon. The sun was shining, the leaves were turning a million colors, and the world seemed like a good place. We sat down by a stream and gazed at the water gurgling over the rocks.

Then we started telling each stories about our families. Carole told me she was really tired of all the moving around, and said her father spent more time with his friends from the army than at home. She said the last move almost caused her parents to divorce.

"Right before we moved here, Mom told Dad, this is it," Carole said, throwing a small stone into the water. "I think she meant it. She said she felt like she was competing with the Pentagon for Dad's affections."

"What did your father say?" I asked her.

"Oh, he promised that he'd try to cut down on his duties and spend more time with us," Carole answered. "But he's said that before. There's always some new excuse why the army needs him to do something in some other city, and off we go again."

"Must be kind of hard for making friends," I said, sympathizing with her.

Carole nodded and then she leaned over and put her head on my shoulder.

Carole's body against mine felt nice. I reached over and rubbed her arm. She grabbed my hand and squeezed it. "I'm glad we're friends," she said.

"Yeah, me too," I answered.

Carole snuggled in closer to me. Her hair smelled of shampoo that reminded me of peppermint candy. And her hand in mine felt soft and warm.

I got a little panicky, wondering if this was the time to make a move with Carole. I tried not to show it, but if Carole noticed anything she didn't seem to care.

"Do you want to have kids when you grow up?" she asked.

"I haven't thought that far ahead," I answered truthfully. "I have enough trouble dealing with my family now." I told her about some of the fights my parents were having. "I don't know." I shook my head. "I wonder if they'll ever be happy. It gets me really upset."

Carole thought for a minute. "Yeah, my parents have their fair share of fights too," she said. "I wonder if people have any idea how happy or unhappy they'll be when they get married. It would be good to know."

I shook my head. "Oh, I'm not sure about that. Why would people get married if they knew they wouldn't be happy?"

"People get married for a lot of reasons. Like security or money."

I thought about Mom and Dad, wondering what had made them get married. I told Carole about the time I asked them, and they acted like they didn't know what to say.

"Maybe they really don't know," Carole said. "Or maybe it's been so long, they've forgotten."

"I suppose that could happen," I agreed. "Life gets petty complicated. Especially when you come to a new country, try to learn a new language, and raise kids on top of all that. Heck, sometimes I can't even remember how I felt last year."

Carole nodded, but didn't say anything. We both sat there quietly, leaning on each other, lost in our own thoughts. Then Carole moved away from me a little and said, "RV. Where are you, RV?" She was staring at me with the funny look that made her eyes sparkle.

"Huh?"

Carole giggled. "You're so far away. We've both been far away. Let's come back here. Here is nice, isn't it?" She moved back a little closer to me.

I hugged her more tightly. Okay, this was it. I leaned over and kissed her on the lips.

Her lips felt soft and spongy, like marshmallows. Except they weren't sweet. They didn't taste like anything. I pulled back, and we were staring at each other again.

"You're a nice guy," Carole said. "I really like you."

"I really like you," I answered. The skin on my face turned hot. I'm sure I was blushing so hard I created new shades of red.

Carole leaned over, wrapped her arms around me, and kissed me so hard, I fell backward onto the grass. Carole fell on top of me and continued kissing me so hard my teeth began to hurt.

Then I felt her tongue against my lips. I'd read about French kissing and knew that you were supposed to let the other person's tongue go into your mouth. The thought of letting someone else's wet tongue in my mouth grossed me out for a second. But this was Carole. It seemed like the right thing to do, so I opened my mouth.

Carole's tongue went right inside, pushing against my tongue, probing around my teeth. I did the same thing, sticking my tongue into her mouth. It was like a sword fight with tongues. I wonder if there's an app that tells you the rules of French kissing. Like whose tongue goes first? Or how much time do you have in the other person's mouth before it's the other person's turn in your mouth? I made a mental note to ask Ray. He's always on his cell phone even at dinner, which makes Dad mad. But if anyone would know about such an app, it would be Ray.

Carole and I lay there kissing and hugging each other. I was starting to get a little tired, but Carole didn't seem tired at all. Her tongue was all over my mouth and my lips, and she was running her hands through my hair.

I figured I better do the same thing, so I started running my hands through her hair. Then I moved my hands over her back, the way James Bond does in his movies. I love James Bond movies, watch all the old ones, and wish they made new ones more often. Now there's a guy who knows how to kiss. I tried to remember all the moves he does with the ladies, but I'm sure my movements with Carole were pretty pathetic compared to his.

Carole finally took her tongue out of my mouth and lifted her head. Her eyes still had that sparkly look in them, though, and she was staring at me for what seemed like hours. Then she finally rolled off me. We lay side by side, looking into the blue sky.

"What are you thinking about?" Carole asked finally.

"Uh, nothing much," I answered. "What are you thinking about?"

"Nothing much."

Carole giggled a little. "Actually, I was thinking this was the best French kiss I've ever had."

I wanted to ask her how many French kisses she had before, but didn't dare.

"How about for you?"

"Oh, yeah. It was great compared to the others," I lied. Am I supposed to admit to her that I've never come close to any kind of kiss with a girl, let alone a French one?

Finally, both of us sat up. "I guess I should be going home," I said, brushing the leaves off my clothes.

"Yeah, I should too," Carole said.

We walked home, not talking too much. I wonder if Carole was thinking about all her French kissing experiences. I was thinking about the opposite—my total lack of kissing experience—in French or any other language.

I kept thinking about it after I'd said goodbye to Carole and made my way to my house. Sure, I was a baby in these things, but it was progress, wasn't it? And I did enjoy myself, even when were played kissy-face with our tongues. So, that was a good sign, right? I was going away from being gay to being straight.

But how much further did I have to go before I really believed it? Opening the back door to our house, I thought about all the apps on Ray's phone. Too bad there weren't any apps to help me deal with that question, were there?

Chapter Seven

God Exists and He Plays Tricks

School is getting harder and harder. There are so many smart kids here! The languages are okay, but science and math are another story. I'm glad I have Carole to help me with algebra. She's so good at it. I don't know who invented adding and subtracting with letters instead of numbers. I mean, really. $x + y = z$. That's warped, if you ask me. Letters are for words. For adding and subtracting you have numbers.

This year our science class is Biology. I'm okay with that. I don't love to cut up frogs or smell formaldehyde, but I'll deal. It's next year's science class I'm worried about. I'll be taking chemistry because I'm going to be a doctor. People say you have to know chemistry to be a doctor.

Surprised that someone like me wants to be a doctor? I didn't say "wants." I said "going to be." Big difference. Mom and Dad are the ones who've decided I'll be a doctor. Well, to be fair, they haven't exactly said it aloud. They're just giving me hints. Strong hints. What they say is, "*Nu, vis nuosis knygoj, Arvydai, Gerai. Būsi daktaru.*" "Your nose is always in a book, RV. Good. You'll be a doctor."

I shrug and go along with it because I'm not really sure what I want to do with my life. If I don't love cutting up frogs, how am I going to deal with cutting up people? On the other hand, doctors make a lot of money, and that's good, isn't it? If I make a lot of money, and give some to Mom and Dad, maybe they'll stop arguing about it so much.

My becoming a doctor isn't the only thing Mom and Dad fantasize about. Other times they say that because of all the books I read I should be a professor. Doesn't sound like a bad profession, getting summers off and everything. But I don't think professors make a lot of money. And besides, I have no idea what subjects I'd teach as a professor. Getting through life being flummoxed? How to get answers from the Big Guy upstairs? How not to screw up your life? Ha! Talk about the blind leading the blind.

I know I shouldn't obsess about my future or what Mom and Dad want for me. I know they sacrificed a lot to come to this country. I know they work hard now. I know, I know, I know! But I work hard too. And it's not like everything is handed to me on a silver platter. And maybe I have problems they don't even know about.

Like gym. I hate gym! Hate it! Hate it! Hate it!

It's probably another sign of being gay, but I can't help it. I have this cretinous a-hole of a gym teacher, Mr. Flaherty. We call him Mr. Flaberty because he's got a big stomach and round red cheeks. I heard people say he used to play minor league baseball. Well, now he looks like he does more eating and drinking than exercising. But he still thinks he's so cool. "Come on. Move it! Move it!" he yells all the time at everybody. "Are you girls or men?"

Flaberty has it in for me. I can tell. He yells at me more than at the other kids. "RV, are you doing jumping jacks or dancing ballet?" "Come on, RV! Hustle, hustle! Are you running or prancing?" "What's with those skinny arms, RV? Show me some bicep!"

That's just when we're just doing exercises. What's Flaberty going to say when I'm out on the field? I can't hit a baseball to save my life. I can't do anything with any ball. Last year some guys in the neighborhood tried to teach me to catch a football. It was humiliating. After we stopped, they were nice and said, "I guess you're right, RV. Maybe you're not cut out to be a ball player." But I saw them whisper to each other and can imagine what they were really thinking. "It's okay, RV. Maybe you're cut out to be a cheerleader." I've heard them say that about other kids.

I don't think I'm a sissy. At least not like Mr. Aniso. I might not be macho, but I'm kind of regular. At least I hope I am. Yes. That's what I want to be—a regular guy. Is that so much to ask for? That's another one of my fantasies. What would it be like to be one of the crowd? For just one day. A regular guy. Not worrying about whether I'm gay or straight. Not feeling different. Not feeling like I don't really belong in the world.

At least I'm not as bad as McGrath. Poor McGrath is not a regular guy. Not by a long shot. He's kind of soft and gay. Not gay as in flamboyant (another great word, though it better not have anything to do with me). McGrath doesn't throw his arms around or screech, but he talks really quietly. Everything about him is gentle, as if you could push him over with a feather. Like I said, soft.

The other day when I was going to my locker, I saw these two guys, Duffy and Doyle, come up to McGrath. They looked around to make sure no one was watching, and then they picked McGrath up and threw him against the lockers so hard everything shook.

"You don't mess with us, you pansy! You got that?"

McGrath turned white and didn't say anything, probably because he was in shock. I don't know what

Duffy and Doyle were mad about, but they picked him up and threw him against the lockers a second time, even harder. Duffy and Doyle are big guys, so when they throw you around, they can do some real damage. I got out of there as fast as I could, before Duffy and Doyle saw me looking and decided to throw me against the lockers too. They're hoods, real hoods. They live in a tough area of Charlestown, which is another part of Boston, and everyone wonders how they got into Latin school. They must be pretty smart. Smart hoods. A scary thought. Did McGrath do something to piss them off? Or do they just hate him because they think he's gay? What do they think of me?

God, if Duffy and Doyle started picking on me, it would be bad news. They'd beat me to a pulp. And I'd get a name for myself at school. Sure, the teachers and some of the kids would act all sympathetic and PC. The teachers would punish Duffy and Doyle (if they dared), but Duffy and Doyle have a way of acting under the radar. They've got the system beat. And I know what some of the other kids would think. I know what they think of McGrath now.

There's a gay club in the school. The Gay/Straight Alliance. You can be straight and be a member, so that way if you're in the club, no one really knows if you're gay. Some kids say they're bi. I've walked by the room where they meet a few times, but I didn't recognize anyone. Of course, I walked by really fast so no one could tell I was interested in what was going on there. So far no one from the club has come up to me or anything, so no one has any clue I might be curious about it. At least I don't think so.

I'm really jealous of the people in the club. How can they be so open and so sure about themselves? I'm not sure about anything. And even if I was, I know how Mom and Dad would react. And not just Mom and Dad, but everyone else in my life. Ray hasn't said anything one way or another, though he's probably a lost cause anyway. I think Carole would be okay, though am I really sure about that? And forget about Jonas S-head and my relatives and Lith acquaintances. They're almost as bad as Duffy and Doyle.

I wish I could figure things out. I wish I weren't so scared. And I wish God would hurry up and answer me instead of taking His sweet time. I've nearly stopped praying a bunch of times. But then every time I stop, I go back to it. I don't know why, but I do. I guess I still want to believe in God. I just wonder if He believes in me.

*

I'm starting to believe God exists. Why? Because He really likes to play tricks on people. Today in Biology class, we had to switch around some seats, and our teacher put me together with Bobby Marshall. The desks in Biology are shared, with two people to a desk. So everyone has a partner. And you get to know your partner pretty well since you're sharing the same microscope, cutting up all those strange animals, writing lab reports, and doing a lot of other stuff together.

I still can't believe Bobby Marshall is my partner. I'm intimidated. (Intimidated. Another word for my favorites list. It means you're scared, but in a more sophisticated way. Kind of like because you're scared you stop yourself from doing things you want to do. When am I going to start finding some more positive words to describe my life?)

Anyway, Bobby Marshall is a jock. A super jock. He's on the junior varsity football team, and he told me he's going to try out for some varsity teams next year. He's good enough. Though he's not big and beefy, like football jocks. He's more regular. Well, not regular, he's still pretty muscular, he's just not the bruiser type. But I can tell he's strong, which I'm sure helps him hold his own against all those big football jocks.

The most amazing thing is, though, Bobby's a nice guy. At least he seems like a nice guy. He doesn't walk around the halls like the other jocks, who have this force field of superiority around them. Like you can't touch them. Bobby seems more down to earth, a regular guy. And he even talks to me in a nice, friendly way.

Oh, and one more thing. He seems pretty smart too. A smart jock who's nice. Does a person like that really exist? I don't know. Me with my suspicious worrying, I'll be waiting for the real, mean Bobby Marshall to come out at some point.

As a matter of fact, I already dreamed about Bobby Marshall once. Yeah, I have to admit I've been a little mesmerized by him ever since school started. So I guess I shouldn't be surprised that I dream about him. In this dream we were having lunch together in the cafeteria, talking about stuff, and everything was nice and friendly. Suddenly Bobby turned scary. His eyes got big and dark and he started sneering at me and calling me names. His football buddies came along and they started calling me names too. And then I woke up.

Am I just being paranoid? Or is that God's way of telling me to stop thinking about Bobby? But then why does He make him my Biology partner? See what I mean about Him playing tricks? I wish I could laugh about it all. Ha ha. But it's easy to laugh when tricks are played on other people. When it's your own life it's not easy at all.

*

I guess this is a good time to admit something else. I do the Big M. Masturbate. I started last year. At least I'm sort of regular that way because I hear other guys at school talk about it doing it too. They do it when they think about girls. I still think about Carole, but now I've started thinking about Bobby Marshall. I picture his face, and how he's so nice and how it feels so good just to be with him, talking about homework in Biology class, looking through the microscope, examining our Petri dishes together. And he has a great smile too. I love it when he smiles at me or makes a joke.

Good old Father Flynn talked about masturbation when he came to talk to the class about sex. At that point, the boys were separated from the girls, and Father Flynn, encouraged us to ask questions, whatever was on our minds. One of the brave kids in class raised his hand and asked, "What about beating off?" Just like that. "What does the Pope say about beating off?"

Father Flynn actually looked a little flummoxed for a second (Yay! Even priests get flummoxed sometimes!). But then he said that he didn't know what the Pope personally thought about masturbation. And he repeated the position of the Church that the purpose of sex is about falling in love and creating a family. That was the highest expression of sex. Father Flynn then talked about the miracle of life, when the sperm in a man's ejaculate joins the egg in the woman's uterus and life is created.

But then someone asked about other forms of sex, maybe not so high but still pretty good. Father Flynn was forced to admit not all the sperm that go into a woman's uterus get to meet an egg and make life.

"A lot of those sperm just swim around in there and don't find an egg to hook up with, right?" one of the kids said. "So what about those poor slobs? They didn't get a chance at making life. That's like masturbation, right?"

In the end it was kind of a standoff. Father Flynn kept emphasizing the Church's position and the highest expressions of sex. But I could tell the other expressions of sex, maybe not the highest but still pretty good, were on everybody's minds.

Of course, no one asked Father Flynn about anything gay. I could picture the expression on his face if I had asked that question. Or the expression on the faces of the other kids. Or my face when Duffy and Doyle started punching me out after school.

No way, Jose. I guess there's a reason why some things aren't talked about.

Chapter Eight

Life Can Be Like Pizza! Sometimes...

Dad came home from work in a really bad mood today. He said they had layoffs. The business at the construction company where he works hasn't been great. A couple of his friends lost their jobs. Dad kept his job, but his pay was cut, even though he has to work the same hours. Which means he'll be even more worried about money and in a worse mood than before.

Dinner was agony. Dad was quiet at first, which made everyone else quiet too. Mom made a special Lith dish: *balandėliai*. "Pigeons." That's what the word means although I have no idea why because the dish has nothing to do with any kind of bird. It's chopped meat wrapped in boiled cabbage. I hate boiled cabbage! And then there are boiled potatoes, which Dad loves. I'm not a big fan of those either. Especially since I'm trying to eat healthier these days and not overdo the carbs. Mom and Dad are big carb lovers though. Bread, potatoes, dumplings—it's the Lith way. With all those carbs in our bodies, it's a wonder my entire family doesn't look like dumplings.

Anyway, we were sitting there eating, with no one saying much of anything. Our typical family dinner. But when I started picking off that boiled cabbage from my meat, Dad became annoyed. I got a lecture about starving kids in Africa and how spoiled we were in this country. Then Dad turned on Ray, who was doing the same thing.

Lucky Ray though. He showed up with a new pair of headphones, so he didn't even hear Dad chew him out. Or if he did, he didn't pay attention.

But that made Dad really mad, and today was no day to make him mad. He grabbed Ray's cell and flung it across the room. Ray jumped up, yelling bloody murder. Dad was about to smack Ray, but Mom intervened. Ray grabbed his cell, cursed at Dad, and ran up to his room.

The three of us tried to finish our dinner. But Dad was worked up now, and started grumbling about the things he usually grumbles about. How we don't appreciate how hard he works for us. How it doesn't matter anyway. How he's not appreciated at work either, or anywhere else. Where have I heard that before? And how often?

Mom had been patient, trying to shush Dad and tell him we'd get by, and things would improve. But his threat to leave must have gotten to her, because she suddenly snapped and told Dad off, saying he should be happy he has a job at all and he should learn to adapt to things the way other people do.

Dad didn't like hearing that and told her maybe he'd be better off leaving the US and going back to the Old Country.

Mom told him he should start packing his bags now so she could find someone else who was better suited to her.

That really got Dad angry. He stood up and started yelling, saying if she ever dared leave him for another man, there would be consequences. "*Supranti?*" he yelled, walking up to her and leaning over so that he was close to her face. "Understand?" I don't know exactly what he meant by consequences, but it didn't sound good.

Mom stood up, backed up a bit, and yelled back at him. I hate it when Mom doesn't back down because it riles Dad up even more. I'm afraid of him when he gets like that, but Mom doesn't seem to care. They both get angrier and angrier, yelling at each other. And then someone throws something, and if they're lucky, one person—usually Mom—runs out of the room before things get worse. And that's what happened tonight. At least Dad didn't hit her.

So there we were, Dad and I, sitting at the table, after Mom had left the room. Neither of us said anything. Dad was frowning and staring straight ahead, putting food in his mouth without paying attention to it.

Sitting alone with Dad when he doesn't say anything is almost worse than when he's grumbling or yelling. You wonder what he's thinking that he can't say. I wish I could ask him, but I can never find the right time. And you get the sense he doesn't want to talk about things anyway.

I was happy when I finally finished my meal and had an excuse to leave the table. I mumbled something about being done, and got up to leave. Dad ignored me.

I went upstairs to my room, leaving Dad behind at the table. But I couldn't forget his face, frowning and staring straight out into space, like he's lost and angry at the same time. It makes me feel the same way, maybe even worse than Dad's feeling. I just wonder if Dad understands that.

*

I have to get to my homework. But I can't start. Even though it was early, I went to bed and lay there. I lay there for a long time, not wanting to move. I was just lying there feeling sorry for myself, asking God why Dad had to have his hours cut, why he and Mom are at each other's throats, and a whole mess of other things that are wrong with my life right now.

Actually, I didn't ask God anything. I cursed Him out instead. Dad grumbles about outsourcing a lot, and now I did it too. Told God He deserved to be outsourced because He was doing a bad job managing the world, especially my world. "You talk about our sins. What about your sins!" I almost shouted.

I know shouting at God is stupid, but it feels good to do it even if it doesn't make Him respond any faster. Maybe He's deaf. Yeah, that's a good one. I mean, look at all those people praying and asking God for stuff over thousands of years. All those millions of words and wails and prayers entering His ears. Maybe it has affected His hearing. Getting a little deaf, are you, God? Or is it that you just don't care?

Oh, oh. I hear someone coming up the stairs. I know those steps. It's Dad. Back to bed. Sorry, God, I didn't mean to call you names. If you're there, if you can hear me—even with one ear—at least don't make things worse than they were at dinner.

*

I'm afraid to look how late it is, but I have to write down what happened when Dad came upstairs. I held my breath when I went back to bed. I thought if I pretended to be asleep, Dad would turn around and leave me alone.

He knocked once, and I didn't respond. But when he knocked a second time and called my name, asking if he could come in, I couldn't stay quiet. So I told him to come in.

Dad opened the door and walked into my room. I was expecting him to be angry, but he looked almost scared.

He stood there looking at me, swaying back and forth a little. I suddenly realized he'd been drinking. Dad drinks, like many people, I guess. Not only with his friends at the Lith Club, but other times too. When I see him drunk, he seems in a good mood, happy and laughing. Not like the stories I hear about other fathers who drink and become mean. Dad becomes nicer. I wish he drank more.

Dad stepped forward, walked up to my bed slowly, and sat down at the other end of the bed. I could smell the alcohol on his breath, even though he was sitting so far away. He sat quietly with his hands together, staring straight ahead, looking the same way he did at dinner.

Then he turned to look at me. I thought he was about to say something, but he looked away again.

"*Atsiprašau,*"he mumbled finally. "*Atsiprašau.*" "I'm sorry."

"That's okay," I said in English. I wanted to kick myself as soon as the stupid words flew out of my mouth. No, it wasn't okay. Nothing was okay. So why did I say that?

Dad turned to look at me again. "*Viskas bus gerai.*" "Everything will be okay." Just like Mom had said to me when she was showing me the jewelry she had made. And just like Mom, I wondered if he was telling me or asking me.

If there was ever an RV frozen moment, this was it. I had never seen Dad like this, looking so defeated. I thought I should say something, but it was as if my brain was shut down. Nothing came out of my mouth. I sat at my end of the bed, afraid to move, almost afraid to breathe. I just wanted him to leave.

Dad was staring straight ahead. Then he reached over, put his hand on my foot, and squeezed it, hard. *"Viskas bus gerai."* He squeezed so hard it hurt. I was about to tell him to stop when he stood up. Swaying even more, he slowly walked out of my room without looking back.

I couldn't move or even think for what seemed like hours. But the image of Dad looking so sad wouldn't leave me. Was he really so scared about his job? About our future? Are things really that bad?

I wish I could go to bed because it's so late, but I don't want to stop writing. I'm getting angry again, angry at all these new things I have to worry about. Hear that, God? Are you testing me? Or are you just having some fun for the heck of it? Well, either way, I wish you'd stop. You've thrown a lot of crap at me, and I think I've dealt with everything okay so far. But it's time for a break, don't you think?

*

Good old Carole. She's there when I need her. She seems to know when I'm feeling really bad. She called me today, asking if I wanted to meet her for pizza. I told her sure, let's go to Joe's. She didn't know about Joe's, so I told her where it was, on a small, out-of-the-way street. The cool kids haven't discovered it. Or maybe they don't like to go there because the clientele is mostly older folks, workmen, and a few people from the neighborhood.

And another thing I like about Joe's: Joe is a nice guy and lets me sit there for as long as I want, reading or thinking about life, munching on my pepperoni or jalapeno slice. Life is good when I'm at Joe's.

That sounded good to Carole. "What's the matter, RV?" she asked me as we sat down at Joe's. "You seem down."

I told her about the fight my parents had yesterday.

"Yeah, it's crappy, isn't it?" Carole nodded. "My parents had a knockdown, drag-out one the other day too."

"So how do you deal with it?" I wanted to know.

Carole shrugged. "I don't know. I try to ignore it."

"But how can you ignore something like that?"

Carole shrugged again. "I just try to think of how my life will be better in the future. Much better."

"That's been my way of dealing with crap too," I said, "but it's getting kind of old. How long am I going to keep living in the future? We have to live now!"

"Look, I'm not saying it's easy, and sometimes it really gets to me too. But if I let it bother me all the time I'd probably be bonkers." She blushed and let out a cute little giggle. "Well, at least more bonkers than I am already."

"You're not bonkers," I answered, laughing. "Not more than me, anyway."

"Good, then we can be bonkers together." She laughed too. "A lot of famous people in history have been bonkers. F. Scott Fitzgerald, who wrote *The Great Gatsby*."

"He wasn't bonkers. His wife Zelda was bonkers."

"Okay. Then how about Albert Einstein?"

"Einstein? He wasn't bonkers. He was a genius!"

"Fine, he was a genius. But a genius can still be bonkers. Have you seen Einstein's picture? Anyone who looks like that has to be bonkers!"

Suddenly Carol looked at her watch. "Oh my God. I have to go. I promised my mother I'd go shopping with her."

She jumped up from the table. "Are you going to stay?"

I nodded. I had bought two slices, and was just starting my second one. I wasn't going to leave before finishing it.

"Okay." Carole gave me a quick peck on the cheek, waved bye to Joe, and ran out the door.

I sat there munching on my pizza. Carole always makes me feel better, even if she doesn't have any solutions to my problems. I guess it's good to know someone else is going through some of the same things you are.

I took my time eating my slice. I didn't want to leave. Sometimes I feel Joe's is more of a home than my own house, especially when Mom and Dad argue. I watched a few people come and go, wondering if they came here to get away from problems the way I did. Most of them looked happy, though, or at least not too miserable. I guess it's hard to be miserable in a pizza parlor.

The door opened and another customer walked in. I looked up. It was Bobby Marshall, my Biology partner.

Bobby looked surprised to see me. Not as surprised as I was to see him.

He looked a little unsure what to do, but then he walked over to my booth.

"Hey, RV," he said.

"Hey, Bobby."

He kind of stood there for a second, looking almost embarrassed. I was embarrassed, too, but finally remembered my manners. "Ah, would you like to sit down?" I said.

"Sure, thanks."

"So, what brings you to Joe's?" I asked. *Duh*. Couldn't I think of something better to say?

Bobby shrugged. "I don't know. I like to come here to think and chill."

"Yeah, me too. I come here with Carole sometimes."

"Carole?"

"Yeah, Carole Higginbottom. The skinny girl with red cheeks. We're friends."

Bobby nodded. "Oh, yeah. She's in some of my classes." Bobby looked away and grew quiet, like he was thinking about something else. But then he turned back to me. "I like this place because not too many people know about it. You can relax."

I nodded. "Yeah." I was glad he said that. For a second I was afraid the cool kids had discovered Joe's, and Carole and I would have to find a new place to hang out.

Bobby looked down at my almost-finished slice of pizza. "Can I get you another slice? That's another reason I come here," he said, finally smiling a little. "I like Joe's combinations."

"Which ones do you like?" I asked Bobby.

"The kale and tomato."

"Oh."

"And the zucchini and squash." Bobby seemed embarrassed again. Maybe because he could see the face I was making. "Yeah, I like vegetables," he said. "Call me a little weird. But they are good on Joe's pizzas."

"That's okay. We're all a little weird," I assured him.

"You're right," he answered, laughing. "And Joe's special combinations make us feel better about it."

Bobby asked me again if I wanted another slice, so I told him to get me a plain cheese one. He went up to the counter to order our slices and some Cokes.

I sat watching him, still finding it hard to believe Bobby was here, hanging out at Joe's.

Doesn't he go to the popular places where everyone else hangs out? I wondered. *He sure doesn't act like a typical jock, does he?*

Bobby came back with a gross-looking slice with green vegetables on it, and my plain one. We sat there eating, not saying very much. This was a different Bobby from the one I knew at school. There he was friendly and talkative, chatting with everybody. But now he was much quieter, into himself. I wondered if he was a little upset that I had intruded on his secret hiding place. I didn't feel he was intruding on mine, but maybe he thought differently.

"So, RV," he said, finally shaking off whatever thoughts were in his head. "What do you like to do for fun?"

Me? Fun? *"I like to read books and learn new words."* No, I couldn't say that. "Oh, you know, I like to do regular things. Like playing ball and stuff." Why did I need to lie?

"You like shooting hoops?"

"Yeah, sure." Another lie. Like maybe I've shot hoops, what, once in my life? And I won't say how many baskets I got.

"So, would you like to come over to my house sometime and shoot some hoops? I've got a nice set-up."

Bobby Marshall inviting me to his house? To shoot hoops?

"Sure, okay." I blushed. "But I'm not that good at basketball. I'm out of practice." I wondered if all those lies were showing on my face.

If they did, Bobby didn't seem to notice. "It's okay, I'm not that good either. Besides this is just for fun, not a competition."

Easy for Bobby to say. But how could I say no to Bobby? Wow! This almost makes up for the terrible few days at home.

*

I'm going crazy. It's almost midnight again, and I've got to stop these late nights, but I can't stop thinking about running into Bobby Marshall today. Is God playing more tricks on me? I'm almost afraid to go to sleep. I'll have another crazy dream where Bobby turns scary and horrible.

Forget dreams. I better worry about reality. I'm scared shitless that Bobby invited me to his house. (I'm not the swearing type, but this moment deserves a swear. And shitless fits perfectly. That's what I am—scared s-h-i-t-l-e-s-s.)

I don't quite get it. Does Bobby really want to be friends? Or was he just being social? But why would he want to be social with me? What's the upside for him?

There's a whopper of a downside for me, isn't there? Once Bobby finds out I know how to shoot hoops about as well as I know Chinese, he'll probably lose all interest in being buddies. Maybe he'll even tell the other kids what a disaster I am, though he doesn't seem that kind of guy.

I better double up on my routine with weights. Yeah, something else on my to-do list this year: bulking up. I ordered a set of weights last summer and have been working out at home. Mom and Dad said I was a fool for spending my money on weights, since I could lift them at school. I tried to explain to them gently that the gym in school isn't exactly friendly territory, and doing a bench press of less than twenty or thirty pounds is considered girlie. Luckily they didn't ask, and I didn't volunteer, that I started my bench presses at fifteen pounds upstairs. Fifteen pounds! That's so pathetic! It's not my fault that I was born with such skinny arms. Another screw-up by my buddy, God. Or maybe it's another one of His tricks, since He seems to have so many of them.

I don't know. Maybe I should just give up; it's obvious I'll never be more macho. My voice still sounds pretty squeaky, no matter how many exercises I do. And I've been practicing the way I move in front of the mirror, trying for more masculine qualities in my life, but I don't think it's helping much. I mean, compared to Bobby Marshall I'm pretty pathetic. I look at him in Biology class, and everything he does is so guy-like. Standing up, sitting down, crossing his legs, talking, even the way he holds his pen when he writes. Guy-ness, regular guy-ness, comes to him so naturally. He doesn't look like he tries at all.

And me? Even if I tried to act like Bobby, I don't think I'd fool anybody. Thank God I'm not like McGrath at least, and no one wants to throw me against the lockers. Not so far, anyway.

Take a breath, RV. There you are, getting down on yourself again and worrying yourself crazy.

Chill out! Chill out! Chill out! You want to go over Bobby's house, don't you? You want to become his friend, right? You might not be a jock, but you're not a complete screw-up either. You'll do fine shooting hoops with him. You can practice a little so you don't make a complete fool of yourself. And anyway what's the worst that can happen if you do? You still have a right to live on this planet, don't you?

Chapter Nine

Holidays Lith Style

I'm sorry I haven't written in a while. It's the holidays, and I hate the holidays! Why? Because my Lith life takes over. My American life disappears. And Bobby Marshall? I haven't had a chance to even think about going over to his house to shoot hoops. That's all on hold too. (Not that I mind so much, of course, since I haven't had time to practice anyway.)

No. Now my family is in full Lith mode, as I call it. First there was Thanksgiving, which is supposed to be the great American holiday, when you eat, drink, and eat some more. For us the great American holiday means getting together with the S-heads, our ritzy, snooty relatives.

The S-heads and our family take turns preparing Thanksgiving, and it was Mom's turn to make the feast this year. She knocked herself out. Even though she's not that close to the S-heads, it's a tradition thing. We've been getting together with them for Thanksgiving for as long as I can remember.

Dad doesn't particularly like the S-heads either, but since the get-together is a tradition thing he doesn't complain, though he usually ends up drinking too much and arguing with Mr. S-head about politics.

At least something different happened at this year's dinner. I put my foot down. I'm still not sure why I did it, but I did.

There we all were, dressed up and sitting at the table with this humongous turkey in the middle that Dad was trying to carve. We were all talking politely about the kinds of things you talk about with relatives, like who died, who got a kidney transplant, and whose rheumatism was bothering them. The kids were trying to be polite, though we usually end up talking in English while the parents talk in the mother tongue. Kind of feels like the United Nations where everyone speaks in different languages and doesn't understand one another. To make it even more fun, sometimes Dad or Mr. S-head throws in a Russian swear word the kids aren't supposed to understand.

Just as we were starting to eat, Jonas Šalinskas mentioned a holiday dance coming up at the Lith Club in South Boston. (Jonas Šalinskas—that's kind of a mouthful. Though it's still not as bad as my full name— Arvydas Aleksandravičius. Try saying that fast three times!) "Are you guys going to go?" he asked.

Before I could answer, Dad said it sounded like a great idea, and that he would drive us.

"But I'm not sure I want to go." The words popped out of my mouth, too fast for me to stop them.

"*Kodėl ne?*" Dad asked, giving me one of those scary looks. "Why not?"

I shrugged. "*Nežinau. Nelabai noriu.*" "I don't know. I don't really want to."

"*Nu, Arvydai. Kodel nutrūkt nuo lietuvybes? Bus smagu.*" That was Mrs. Šalinskas. She's got beautiful blonde hair and expensive clothes and like I said, she's a big activist in Lith immigrant affairs. She was asking me why I was distancing myself from my heritage. That word again.

Before I could answer, Miss Beautiful Jolanda agreed with her mother, saying there would be a live band.

"Cool. We should go." That was Ray, who's usually the quietest person at these dinners. He was being polite tonight, though, because I think he has a crush on Jolanda.

"Yeah, it should be great," Jolanda and Jonas said at the same time. "Come on, RV. Don't be a party pooper. There'll be great dancing."

I thought back to the last time Jonas convinced me not to be a party pooper at the concert where I threw up. And I got mad all over again. I told everyone as nicely as I could stand it that dancing and partying were just not my things. That's not totally true, but for some reason I said it.

Dad gave me another dirty look and Mrs. S-head harrumphed, telling everyone she'd keep after me until I agreed to go.

Good old Mom tried to change the subject, saying we could talk about it later. But Mrs. S-head got onto her high horse, giving us a lecture on why maintaining tradition and one's culture was so important. That word just doesn't go away, does it? It pleased Dad, and he agreed. But that didn't please Mom, who said kids should have a choice too. Then Mr. S-head, who'd been quiet so far, piped up, asking me what I had against the dance.

I wasn't about to tell him what his son convinced me to do at the concert, though I was sorely tempted to. I said I just wasn't interested. I guess I said it a little too emphatically because Dad got mad, telling me to apologize for being so impolite. Even Mom looked a little upset, but she still told Dad to stop picking on me.

Dad got angrier, telling Mom to butt out. Mr. and Mrs. S-head looked embarrassed. The kids rolled their eyes.

I wanted to run away from the table. But we had to finish the meal. Luckily, for once, Mom didn't answer Dad back but just turned away and let it go. Dad poured himself a drink, dismissing the discussion with a wave of his hand and getting into his kids-are-ungrateful routine. That started them on politics, and he and Mr. S-head started talking about the latest thing the Russians were doing.

*

So that's a typical holiday dinner at our house. Lovely, isn't it? I wish I knew why I said I didn't want to go to the dance in front of everybody. And even more I wish I knew why I didn't want to go. Dances aren't the worst thing in the world. I've gone to some before, and they were okay. So why does this feel different? Am I still really so mad about what happened at the stupid concert?

Maybe I've already had enough of the holidays. Thanksgiving was just the start. Now we have Christmas, and I know what's coming for Christmas.

First is helping the orphans in the Old Country. That's Dad's thing. I have nothing against orphans and think it's a very good idea. It's just Dad overdoes it as usual.

First there's a toy drive. Then a push to get medical supplies. Then food and clothing. Dad drives all over the city, collecting everything, which is then deposited in a holding center of a relief organization to be packed up and sent to the Old Country.

Oh, and he has to do one more thing. He has to organize the volunteers. Sometimes Dad gets a lot of friends to help out. Sometimes just a few. Lately it's been just me.

I use the word "volunteer" loosely, as the adults say. Dad asked me to help a few years ago, and I was all too happy to help. In those days I was still pretty tight with the Big Guy upstairs, wanting to be holy, doing good deeds, and feeling like my prayers were listened to, if not always answered.

But now it's getting a little old. I still believe in good deeds, but with Dad it's like being in the army. Get up early, drive all around town, lug heavy boxes, pack, wrap, label. You would think it's some kind of marathon. I asked Dad once why he did this and all he said is "Because it's important not to forget those less fortunate." That's nice, but why not Haiti or Bangladesh, where people are worse off than in Europe? I think it has something to do with the family Dad left behind. Maybe there's even an orphan somewhere in the family, though Dad's never mentioned one.

And then there's Mom's version of the holidays. First is church. I've started calling Mom "Super Catholic" because she's getting more religious, volunteering at church and going to Mass during the week sometimes. And of course she makes us go to the Lith Mass on Sunday mornings, which is in a church in South Boston. If we complain, she tells us it's important to support the church, that not enough people go. "What's wrong with an American church?" Ray asks. "Isn't God the same everywhere?" Apparently not to Mom. She says the church helped her a lot when she was a young girl in Lithuania, and it needs our support.

So we go.

But that's not all. Mom also helps put on a Christmas pageant every year, at the Litsky school. Mom teaches there. Parents bring their kids there from all around Boston to learn everything about the Old Country. Ray and I had to set a good example, being a teacher's kids and all, so for years we had to be in these Christmas pageants whether we wanted to or not. I've been an elf, a reindeer, a bear, a tree, a snowflake, and a lot of other things. I finally stopped doing it a couple of years ago after I had to be a mushroom.

Luckily Mom bowed out of the pageant this year. I know Ray was going to finally put his foot down on that, too, and say "no more." But it's one fight he didn't have to have because Mom's now busy concentrating on her jewelry business. She's doing it to earn some extra cash since Dad's bringing in less money. She joined a website where she can sell her jewelry. Carole, Tim, and I are helping her with the computer part. Mom's excited, though Dad is a little nervous that somehow she'll be taken in by scammers. But Carole told him not to worry. She explained about PayPal and other protections. I don't think Dad understood too much because he just mumbled something and walked away. But at least he hasn't been complaining about it at dinner.

*

To tell the truth, holidays at school are no great shakes either. We have all these end-of-term tests I have to study for, so who has time for the Christmas spirit? I think I'm doing okay, in most classes anyway, so I shouldn't worry, but you never know. With all these genius kids running around, I don't feel so smart.

In grammar school, being smart helped me get over those bad days when kids called me names. Having a good brain does heal some of the wounds made by the slings and arrows of misfortune. (I just learned that phrase. "The slings and arrows of misfortune." It makes the crap in your life sound so much more important, doesn't it?)

But here at Latin school I don't stand out because there are a lot of smart and smarter kids running around. So in that way, I fit in. I kind of like being one of the crowd and I don't. I thought I always wanted to fit in, be a regular guy and all that, but now that I do, I feel a little weird. Almost scared. Isn't that crazy? What am I afraid of now? It's like part of me always wants to fit in and part of me doesn't. Man. Is this another trick of the Big Guy upstairs? I thought things were supposed to make more sense when you got older, but here's another thing to figure out about myself. When's it going to stop?

*

Well, the Big Guy upstairs is at it with his tricks again. Today in Biology class, before the teacher came in, I saw a couple of kids talking and laughing by the desk of Louie Whalen. Whalen is another one of these smart, quiet guys, but he has a sense of humor so it's fun to hang around with him. I do, too, sometimes. Today, though, when the kids by Whalen's desk laughed, they looked over at me. I asked them what the matter was. One of the kids grabbed a piece of paper out of Whalen's hand and showed it to me. Whalen likes to draw, and today he drew a couple of figures with exaggerated features and put names underneath them to show they represented certain people in class. One guy was fat, and another guy had food dribbling out of the side of his mouth. I was there as well.

My figure had a halo above it and wings coming out of the side. It was an angel.

RV the Angel. Drawn by Whalen, who's not exactly a cool kid himself. Am I so bad? Even Whalen sees me as an angel? How long is it going to take for me to live that down? (Though the crazy things is, if they only knew!)

Well, I guess I don't fit in as much as I thought I did. Thanks, Big Guy. So what are you trying to tell me now? I shouldn't try to fit in in the first place? I should just accept the good and the bad and stop worrying?

At least Bobby Marshall wasn't in class at the time. If he had seen the drawing of RV the Angel, I wonder how he would have reacted. He still mentions shooting hoops together, but he's been really busy since he said it. Now that football is over, Bobby is busy with junior varsity hockey and basketball. Is there any sport this guy isn't good at? Fine with me if he wants to put me off. I can wait. It will give me more time to bulk up my puny arms.

*

What a joke! I was upset about being called an angel the other day. But that's nothing. Today in school I saw something much worse—and what you can do about it.

Duffy and Doyle, those scary hoods who throw people against lockers, were transferred to Mr. Aniso's Latin class a few weeks ago. Who knows what they did in someone else's class or why some bureaucratic moron thought Mr. Aniso could handle both of them at the same time, but they are here now. Sitting right behind me.

Luckily, they've kind of been nice to me—so far anyway. As a matter of fact, they haven't picked on any of the kids in class. That's because they have too much fun picking on Mr. Aniso. They mimic his voice when he calls on them. They make their wrists go limp when they raise their hands. And they say "swish, swish," in really high voices whenever he walks by. I can't believe he doesn't hear them. Or maybe he just pretends not to.

Today, though, Mr. Aniso heard them—or he had enough. He walked by and when Duffy said "swish swish," Mr. Aniso stopped and turned around.

"What did you say, Mr. Duffy?"

"Me?"

"Yes, you."

"I didn't say anything, sir."

"Oh no? Then who said 'swish, swish'?"

"Swish, swish?"

"Yes. Swish, swish."

Everyone was tense except Duffy, who was trying not to laugh. Doyle snickered. Mr. Aniso then turned to him. "Do you think this is funny, Mr. Doyle?"

"No, sir."

"Do you, Mr. Duffy?"

"No, sir."

"Good. Then to make sure you've both been paying attention, both of you will read through the end of Chapter Five in your textbooks tonight. And tomorrow, after the last bell, you will report here for a quiz, so I can make sure you understand the material."

Mr. Aniso turned around and began to walk away.

"Faggot. Fucking faggot!'" Doyle said under his breath.

Mr. Aniso turned around. "Mr. Doyle. Stand up."

Doyle did as he was told. He's a big guy, so when he stood up he was as tall as Mr. Aniso.

Mr. Aniso walked up to him so he was just a few inches away from Doyle's face.

"What did you say, Mr. Doyle?"

"Nothing."

"I heard something."

Doyle didn't say anything.

"I heard the word 'faggot,' Mr. Doyle," Mr. Aniso said. "As well as a swear word to go with it. Did you say faggot?"

"No, sir." Doyle didn't sound convincing.

"I think you did, Mr. Doyle. I think you said it to insult me. Do you think it's a good way to insult me—or anyone else?"

Doyle just stood there, staring at Mr. Aniso. Mr. Aniso stared back at him. Everyone was so quiet, I think they were hardly breathing. We were all wondering what would happen next.

Mr. Aniso let out a breath. "Do you know what the penalties are for insulting a teacher, Mr. Doyle? If you want another mark toward detention, I can easily supply you with one. But we will deal with that later. First things first. Tomorrow night, after the quiz, we will have a discussion on why you think you can insult anyone by calling them a faggot."

Doyle didn't say anything.

"Is that clear?"

Doyle mumbled something under his breath.

"I said, is that clear?"

"Yes, sir," Doyle finally said in a louder voice.

Mr. Aniso turned to Duffy who had started making a face.

"And you still think this is funny, Mr. Duffy?

"No, sir," answered Duffy, swiftly trying to look serious.

Mr. Aniso didn't buy it. "Mr. Duffy, you can stay with Mr. Doyle after the quiz and participate in the discussion.

I will see both of you after the last bell." Then Mr. Aniso turned around and walked back to the font of the class.

Doyle swore under his breath. "Fucking faggot." I heard Duffy swear too. I was praying really hard that this time Mr. Aniso didn't hear it.

As soon as the bell sounded I ran out of the class. I don't want to be anywhere near the class tomorrow night. Mr. Aniso standing up to Duffy and Doyle? Wow. I couldn't believe it. Still can't, not really. Where does he get the courage to take them on? He might seem soft and swishy on the outside, but inside I guess he's not swishy at all.

Chapter Ten

You Cannot Be Who You Are Not

Bobby Marshall and I are shooting hoops tomorrow. Bobby called me up out of the blue today and asked me if I had time to come over. The holidays are over, he has a break from practice, and the weather will be good. So I said "sure."

"Sure." Sounds so nonchalant. (Nonchalant. Another great word. I learned it over Christmas. It means you don't care, but in a kind of French, European way.) That fits perfectly for me. "Sure, Bobby. I'll shoot hoops with you." Like I'm French and it means nothing to me to get a few baskets. Ha, ha. In reality, I am nervous as hell.

Am I swearing again? Yes, but it's how I feel. Have to get the bad feelings out sometimes, right?

I tried to forget about Bobby and playing hoops during the holidays, but it was on my mind all the time. I even tried to watch some basketball games on TV with Dad. Dad loves basketball. It's the national sport of the Old Country, and he's tried to get me interested in the game for the longest time.

But I could never get into it. During Christmas break, though, I gave it another try. A real try. One night I went downstairs and sat with Dad as he watched the Boston Celtics. Dad seemed surprised but happy—maybe his weird son was turning over a new leaf?

"*Gerai. Gerai.* Good, good. Important to know more than books." There Dad was again, trying to bond with me in his stupid English. He tried to tell me about the strategy of the game, but the more he talked, the more I wanted to run upstairs and go back to the book I'm reading.

"Sorry, Dad. You like 'em basketball. Me like 'em books." I didn't really say that, but I wanted to. I know I'm being mean, but I just wish he'd stop trying to talk to me in English and pretend to be something he's not.

I wonder why so many fathers do that, trying to be like their sons, when they're obviously different. Maybe they think it's a way to be closer. And being close to their sons is part of the job, the Dad job. If it is, they should rewrite the job description.

I shouldn't be so hard on Dad. I'm trying to be something I'm not, too, aren't I? After all, I was the one who went down and watched the game with him, even though I don't really care about it. It's all to prove something to Bobby Marshall, isn't it?

I have to admit something else as well. After Dad went to bed, I snuck back down and turned on the TV again. The basketball game was over, but there was a hockey game on.

I tried to watch the game and get into it, but that was boring too. All those guys without teeth skating around on the ice and hitting one another with sticks did not get me excited. I wish I could explain it, but I can't. I'm reading *Crime and Punishment* now and that's so much more interesting to me. This guy, Raskolnikov, kills an old woman, who he says is useless to the world. He thinks he won't feel guilty, but he does. It's all about how guilt eats you up. I can relate to that. Of course I haven't killed anyone and I don't think I ever will, but all the stuff about guilt is really good. I'm taking pointers.

I don't suppose Bobby Marshall thinks about guilt when he's shooting hoops. He doesn't look like he feels guilt about anything. Why can't I be like him?

There I go again. Stop it, RV! Stop putting yourself down! You'll just have to go out there and do your best. And whatever baskets you get will be fine.

That's the school spirit, as Flaberty, our gym teacher, keeps reminding us—over and over. Maybe he's right about that. Don't give up. I've never been known to shirk responsibility, right? Even if I'm nervous, I'll go to Bobby's and will be nonchalant, just like the French. If I can even make one basket, that will be great. And who knows, maybe I'll do better. Maybe I'll even become friends with Bobby.

*

You are not a jock. Repeat. You are not, and never will be, a jock.

I'm exhausted. I just want to crawl into bed and sleep—for a long time. But I have to write down what happened at Bobby's house this afternoon, so I don't make an ass of myself again.

Bobby lives in a nice big yellow house with his parents. They look like the rich, polite types. They invited me in when I got there, and we all sat in the living room making the kind of brainless conversation one usually has in living rooms. After a while, Bobby said it was time to go outside.

Before I knew it, he was dribbling the ball like a pro and getting one basket after another. He would send the ball to me too. I tried to throw it into the basket but I missed almost every time. When Bobby threw the ball, it seemed so easy for him. When I did it my movements were clumsy and I probably looked like a clod. The hoop is attached to the garage, and once the ball bounced off the wall and went flying into the side of their expensive-looking car, which was parked at the side of the driveway. I was glad his father wasn't around.

After a few minutes of this farce, which felt like hours to me, Bobby could probably tell I wasn't really enjoying myself. "Here, RV," he said, coming up to me. "Can I give you a few pointers?" At least he didn't say, "You stink."

"Here, hold the ball like this and stand like that," he said, taking the ball and acting like he was about to throw it. Then he gave me the ball, and I tried to do that too. I put one hand up over the ball, and the other one under it, and pushed my legs apart like Bobby did. "Hmmm," Bobby said. "That's kind of right, but try to relax. Why are you tense?"

Why was I tense? Take three guesses, Bobby, and the first two don't count. But I tried to do as Bobby suggested. I moved my feet apart more, and tried not to hold onto the ball so tightly. But then I couldn't move and it felt like the ball was going to drop out of my hands.

Bobby shook his head. "No, no. Too much. A little looser. Don't tense up. Just focus on the hoop."

Easy for Bobby to say. "If I focus on the hoop I won't see what my hands are doing."

"You don't need to see your hands. Your brain will guide them."

Maybe Bobby's brain works that way, but not mine.

I tried to follow Bobby's instructions, focusing my eyes not on the ball or my hands, but on the hoop above the garage door. Bobby seemed pleased. "Good. Good. Just throw the ball. Look at the hoop and the ball will follow."

But the ball didn't follow. No matter what I did, it seemed to have a mind of its own, going everywhere except where I wanted it to. And my brain didn't help. Bobby tried all sorts of things, even standing in front of me and instructing me to mimic his actions step by tiny step. I did, over and over, but it just didn't work for me.

Bobby's father came out and began trying to coach me too. He's probably forty, or even older, but his throws were even better than Bobby's. That just screwed me up totally. Now I had two people witness my incompetence, including someone that old. My throws started getting worse, and I hit the car again. A couple of times the ball bounced off the wall of the garage right onto the car's windshield.

The last time it did, I thought I heard a crack. A loud crack. We all stood there holding our breath. Bobby walked over to the car, and looked at the windshield. "No harm done," he said. "It was just a branch on the windshield that the ball hit." He turned back to us. "Wow, RV. You've got quite an arm. For baseball," he added with a grin.

"I'm sorry," I said miserably. "I guess I'm just not cut out for this."

Bobby shook his head. "That's okay. I'm not good at a lot of things."

"Name one," I wanted to tell him but didn't dare. His father seemed relieved when Bobby suggested we finish the game. We went inside, and his mother offered us some snacks. We made some more living room chitchat, and then at the first opportunity I told them I had to go.

"Before you go, can you do me a favor?" Bobby asked.

"Sure," I answered, hoping I could make up at least a little bit for my lousy hoop shooting.

Bobby said he needed some help with an essay we had to write for English class. I followed him to his room, and gave him a few pointers.

"Thanks," he said, reading it over when we were done. "This is so much better."

Wow! Something I can do better than Bobby Marshall! That made me feel a little bit more cheerful, and I was happy to see Bobby looking pleased.

But I still couldn't wait to get out of there. Making some excuse about needing to be home, I got on my bike and left.

So much for trying to be a jock. Cycling home, I remembered a homeless man I had seen once when I'd gone into Boston with my parents. He was wandering up and down the street shouting, "You cannot be who you are not. You cannot be who you are not!" At the time we all hurried by and ignored him. But now his words hit home, like they were directed at me.

Another little lesson of life. I just wish these lessons didn't hurt so much.

*

"I'm kind of down."

"Why? What's the matter?"

"I think my parents are really splitting up this time."

"What makes you say that?"

"I heard them talking, and they both said they'd probably be better off alone."

"Maybe it was just talk."

"I don't think so. They sounded serious. They weren't even fighting."

It was Carole. She called me on the phone this afternoon, asking me if I'd go to Joe's for a slice of pizza with her. She wanted to talk in person.

"I just wanted to get out of the house," she admitted, when we sat down with our pizza slices. "I needed to be with someone who's not my parents." Carole's mother has been sick, so Carole has been stuck at home a lot, helping around the house. She hasn't even had much time to devote to our computer business.

"How's your mother doing?" I asked.

"She's better, physically at least. But mentally she's gone wacko. She picks on me for every little thing."

"Really?"

"Yeah. She can be a real bitch." Carole blushed. I guess she feels the same way I do when she swears. Why is it so important for us to think of ourselves as good kids? Are we trying to prove something?

I wanted to hug Carole, but I patted her hand instead.

"It's okay. Maybe it's because she's going through a rough time with your father."

"Maybe. But that's still no excuse."

"And how's your father?"

Carole shrugged. "He's fine. When he's home. But that's hardly ever."

I felt really bad for her. She seemed very unhappy. "Maybe then it's better if they do split up," I said, trying to think of something positive to say. "Maybe it will be better for everybody."

Carole shrugged again, staring off into space. "Maybe." She didn't look convinced.

"And how are you doing?" she asked, looking up at me.

"I'm okay." I told her about trying to shoot hoops with Bobby Marshall. "That will teach me to be a jock."

That made Carole smile. "I like you even though you're not a jock."

Now it was my turn to blush. "I'm glad someone likes me."

"I like you a lot," Carole said. "If one of us moved away, how would we run the business alone?"

"Neither one of us is going anywhere," I said.

Carole perked up. "You know, we have to get our business going again. I know I've let it go, and Tim's been busy too. But the holidays are over, and maybe people will be thinking about their computers again."

"Maybe they got new ones for Christmas. Or phones. Or tablets."

"Great idea! We need to advertise again! Maybe take things in a different direction." Now Carole was her old self, as we sat and discussed what other things we could do with our business. It made me feel better too.

We left Joe's and walked home through the woods by the ball field to our favorite spot, still discussing the business. Then Carole looked up. "It's snowing," she said.

I looked up too. A few small snowflakes hit my face, and then they got larger as it started snowing harder.

I took hold of Carole and wrapped my arms around her, hugging her tight. I was glad she was my friend, and I was glad we were there to talk to each other, whenever we needed it.

"Look. It's so beautiful." Carole hugged me back and gazed out into the distance. The snow was covering everything we could see—the field, the brook, the trees in the woods behind us, and the hills in the distance.

"It looks like a postcard," I said. I wanted to stand there and hold her for a long time, enjoying the snow and how it made everything white and silent.

But then Carole shivered. "I need to warm up. Do you want to come to my house before you go home? I'll make us a cup of hot chocolate."

That sounded good, since I was getting cold too.

We went back to Carole's house, where we took off our coats and shoes, and made ourselves comfortable in the living room. Carole went off to the kitchen to make some hot chocolate, and I sat down on a long sofa.

Carole's house was big, bigger than mine, but it seemed so empty and quiet. "Where is everybody?" I wanted to know.

"Mom's out shopping and Dad's away for work," Carole called back from the kitchen. "I told you, Dad's hardly around."

I sat on the sofa wishing she'd hurry up with the hot chocolate. I was still cold, and I realized it was because some of the snow had fallen down my neck and soaked the collar of my shirt.

Finally Carole came out of the kitchen with two mugs. "Mmm, that smells good," I said, shivering a little. I picked up one of the mugs, letting the hot steam hit my face. Carole picked up the other mug and sat down next to me.

The hot chocolate tasted delicious. "Mmm... Mmm..." we both said, sipping from our mugs.

I shivered again. The hot chocolate was warming my stomach but it made my wet shirt collar feel even colder.

"What's the matter?"

I showed Carole the collar. "Oh, it's wet," she said. "Here, let's take it off and dry it."

She put down her mug, and before I could say anything she had me unbutton my shirt and helped me take it off. She put it on the back of a chair and came back down to sit beside me.

She was giggling. "Nice arms," she said.

"Yeah, right. Puny arms."

My wet shirt was off, but I was still cold sitting there in my undershirt.

I rubbed my arms, trying to get rid of the goose pimples that were forming. "Here. It's my turn to hug you," Carole said. She moved closer and started rubbing her hands over my arms. "Does that feel better?" she asked. She was getting a familiar look in her eyes again. The sparkly, excited look I remembered from the time we French kissed by the brook.

"Ahh, sure... Yes," I answered, trying to sound confident.

Carole continued rubbing my arms. The sparkly, excited look in her eyes got even more sparkly. Then she leaned over and kissed me on the lips.

Before I knew it, I was kissing her back, and rubbing my hands all over her. We started French kissing, and this time our tongues were a little more coordinated, moving in and out of our mouths without bumping into each other constantly.

I started to relax. Then Carole moved back and said her blouse was wet too. And she took it off. Right there in front of me.

She was wearing a bra with red and black polka dots.

"Do you like it?" she asked, giggling a little and pointing to her bra.

What do you say when a woman asks you if you like her bra? "Nice polka dots."

Carole giggled again. "It's okay," she said. "You can look at my bra. But that's as far as we go."

I nodded, not knowing whether to look or not. I'd never seen a woman in a bra before. Not one who was sitting a few inches away from me.

Carole giggled and then kissed me. She moved back and said, "This is nice."

"Yes, nice," I said. Carole's eyes still had that sparkly, excited look about them. My eyes probably had a look of terror.

We started kissing again. Then Carole ran her hands over my shoulders and back, and I did the same to her. Then we lost our balance and fell down on the sofa.

Our lips were still locked together and my hands were pinned under Carole, who was lying underneath me. Neither of us could move. I wasn't sure what to do, but Carole wriggled out from under me, so she was lying beside me. She turned her head and whispered in my ear. "I like you, RV. I like you a lot."

"I like you too," I said.

We began kissing again. I couldn't believe this was happening. I was a regular guy, making out with a girl. A girl who even let me see her bra. Maybe for the first time in my life I didn't feel like I was different at all. I was a guy like other guys. It was fantastic.

After a while, we stopped kissing again. Carole tilted her head back, held my head in her hands, and gazed into my eyes. The sparkly, excited look hadn't gone away.

She kept gazing into my eyes, though she didn't say anything. I didn't say anything either. But we didn't have to speak. We were just happy looking into each other's eyes. And I know we both wanted the make-out session to continue forever.

*

I'm *so* happy. We had a real make-out session, didn't we? Me, RV! Making out with a girl. Wow! Flaberty is really right! You gotta have hope. And it will work out.

So maybe that homeless guy was wrong after all. You can be who you are not. Or maybe I'm not gay and this is the real me. Why was I so worried?

Whatever it is, I'm just happy tonight. Let me forget trying to figure things out and just go to bed happy for once.

PS: If you had anything to do with this, God, thanks. For the snow and for Carole inviting me to her house. You do work in strange but wonderful ways.

Chapter Eleven

Family Dinners Are Not All Alike

Wow, what a great start to the new year. Carole and I have been getting together whenever we can to make out. We usually go to her house because her parents aren't home often. It feels good to lie on the sofa, kiss, and feel her up.

Carole likes it too. Maybe more than me because she moans and groans a lot.

"Oh, RV. Yes."

"Mmmm."

"Don't stop, RV."

"Kiss me."

It's a little scary, actually, all this talking during our make-out sessions. Carole says she's never gone this far with a guy before, but I'm not so sure. With all those words, she sounds like she's been around the sofa once or twice. And she has this great collection of bras. Last week she wore one with a zebra pattern. And the other day she had this frilly thing on, like she was from another century or something. I never knew bras came in so many different colors and designs.

Whatever. I'm just happy. Making out with a girl and feeling her up like other guys do. Wow! I still can't believe it.

So all my worrying about being gay was just that, right? Worrying. In good, old RV fashion. Worrying when I didn't have to worry. I still think about Bobby a lot, but when I'm feeling up Carole, I can even forget about him for a time. I know I have to chill out. Sometimes life does work out. I should really start believing that.

Even our crazy family dinners aren't enough to spoil my good mood these days. Now, when Mom and Dad are fuming at each other or Ray is saying something obnoxious, I have this urge to say, "Mom, Dad. How was your day? I was with Carole. We made out on her sofa. She has a great collection of bras."

I wonder what Mom and Dad would do? Of course I could never ask them. I wonder why that is—why people don't talk about making out publicly. At least not often. Especially adults. Is that because they think it's embarrassing? Or private? Why is something private or embarrassing? Is it because it's wrong? Or just something people want to keep to themselves because it's special?

I guess I wouldn't want to hear about Mom and Dad talking about that kind of stuff. So I suppose it's only fair they don't want me talking about it either. Okay, it's a deal as far as I'm concerned. I'll just keep what I do to myself—and Carole.

*

Nothing like one of our family dinners to put me in a bad mood again.

Today we got a call from the principal at Ray's school. He goes to the same grammar school I did, a Catholic school run by nuns. The principal there is Sister Helen Dorothy. There's a special name for her too: Sister Hell Dog. When Sister Hell Dog calls you know you're in trouble. She didn't even want to talk to Mom, asking to speak to Dad right as we were starting dinner. She told him she wanted Dad to come down to the school with Ray so they could all have a talk in her office. Some equipment was missing from one of the school's storerooms, and she suspected Ray and his best friend might know something about the matter. She wanted to discuss other bad behavior too.

Dad told us all this after he put down the phone. We all looked at Ray. A few weeks ago, he started sporting those new headphones. He told us he had won them in a school lottery. His story didn't sound too likely, but no one challenged him on it. Now, though, I think we were all wondering the same thing.

"*Nu*? Well?" Dad looked really angry.

"What?"

"*Tai to betrūko? Mano sunus vagis*?" Dad was pretty much accusing him of being a thief.

"I told you. There was a school lottery..." Gotta hand it to Ray. No matter how much trouble he's in, he only talks to Dad in English.

"*Kalbėk lietuviškai!*" No surprise, that made Dad even angrier, and he insisted on the mother tongue.

"*Shh, nerėk!*" Mom was on edge, too, telling Dad not to yell and give Ray a chance to explain himself.

Dad was about to say something to Mom, but then turned silent and ran his fingers through his hair. His hair used to be jet-black, but I just noticed it's getting some gray in it. A lot of gray in places.

Mom turned away from him and looked at Ray. She asked him about the headphones in a quiet voice, almost like she was showing Dad how it should be done. But Ray told her the same story he's been giving us all along.

That got Mom mad too. "*Nemeluok man!*" she said to Ray. "Don't lie to me!"

"*Aš nemeluoju!* I'm not lying!"

Mom turned silent, looking a little embarrassed. Dad turned to her. "*Dabar ka?* Now what?" he said in a mocking voice.

Mom didn't say anything, turning her gaze away from him. I'm sure it's hard for parents when they feel their kid is out of control.

"*Reikia diržo, o ne ko kitko!*" Dad exclaimed, pointing to his belt and looking at Ray angrily. We all knew what he meant.

But Mom didn't let that go. She's big on talking to people, so she tried to convince Dad to forget about the belt and reason with Ray. Dad said the time for reasoning was over. "*Reikia tvarkos.*" That's another one of his favorite expressions. "We need order."

They went back and forth like that for a while, and I just sat there, frozen as usual. Finally I couldn't take it anymore. I jumped and ran upstairs to my room, leaving Mom and Dad arguing over the table and Ray still sitting there with a smirk on his face.

How Ray could sit there and not care about any of this is beyond me. Even though I was upstairs I couldn't forget what was happening downstairs. And yet he was right there in the table in the middle of it—no, the cause of it— and he was able to shrug it off. How? What kind of genes did he get that I missed out on?

I spotted a face staring at me in the doorway. "Great family. Aren't we?"

It was Ray.

"Just get out of here!"

"What's the matter?"

"You know what's the matter."

"No. You know what's the matter. Don't blame me for Mom and Dad overreacting."

"You took stuff from school! That's bad."

"Don't give me that goody-goody Big Brother routine. You're just like them."

Ray turned around and left, but not before giving me a look and adding, "And I did not take stuff from school."

I wanted to believe him, but I couldn't. Not then, not now. I hate Ray sometimes. The last thing we need is another fight in this family. Why does he have to cause more problems?

*

I WILL NOT LET MY FAMILY GET TO ME.
I WILL NOT LET MY FAMILY GET TO ME.
I WILL NOT LET MY FAMILY GET TO ME.

I know it's not good to hate your family, but I can't think of anything else at the moment. I can't focus on anything else, so I've been sitting here writing that stupid sentence over and over.

I guess what I'm most mad about is that it feels like they're trying to bring me down. I was feeling so good about everything, and then I have to come home and deal with this. My mood changes so fast. Maybe my family doesn't mean to bring me down, but they do. They f$*!#!!*#-ing do!

I'm swearing again. Good. Maybe that shows how bad I'm feeling. And the more I think about what happened tonight, the worse I feel. The fucking assholes. The fucking, fucking assholes.

I'm not going to let them though. I'm not going to let them bring me down. I may be screwed up in a lot of ways, but I'm doing okay in other ways. Is this another one of your tricks, Big Guy? You finally make me feel better about myself, and then you remind me that some parts of my life—big parts—are still screwed up.

Is that how life works? Well, that's great.

But I'm not going to accept it. I don't know what I can do about it at the moment, but I just can't accept it.

*

I couldn't write for a while because I was feeling so down, but now I have to write about something good again. I guess that's how life really does work. Up and down. Up and down. And the Big Guy is pulling the strings. I just have to accept it.

Bobby Marshall invited me to his house last weekend, saying he had another essay he needed help with. Even though I still feel bad about how I made a fool of myself shooting hoops with him, I guess he doesn't care about it too much. I was a little nervous when I went over, and was already thinking about some non-lame excuses I could come up with in case he wanted to shoot hoops again, but he never mentioned hoops. And I didn't have to make polite chitchat with his parents in the living room either. Instead we went right up to his room and he showed me the essay. It was on a history book he had read about the presidents. He had to do a report on it, but he was having trouble putting down what he liked or didn't like about the book.

I gave him a few tips. "That's what I admire about people like you," Bobby said, looking up from his paper. "You're so good at expressing yourself, at explaining what you think."

Me? Expressing myself? That was kind of a joke, but if Bobby said it, maybe he really meant it.

I sat at his desk, wondering about Bobby's compliment, when he said, "So what do you think?"

"Huh?"

"Hey, RV. Are you not paying attention?"

"Oh, I'm sorry," I apologized. I'm sure I was blushing my thousand shades of red.

Bobby was smiling though. "Hey, I know the book is boring. But I need your help."

"Sure. I was just thinking about other stuff."

"Well, think about other stuff later. I need more help on what to say about the book."

I tried to concentrate and started reading Bobby's paper again. But it was getting late so we agreed to meet again the next day after he came home from practice.

The next day was Saturday, and his parents were both home. They invited me to dinner after I helped Bobby finish his paper. Mom and Dad said it was fine, so I said yes.

Dinner was fancy, fancier than we have at home. I wasn't surprised, given how big and upscale Bobby's house was. Everyone acted really nice and seemed in a good mood. Bobby was in a good mood, too, and only got annoyed once when his father mentioned one of Bobby's junior varsity trophies.

"Dad, stop it. RV doesn't want to hear about trophies."

"Oh, Bobby. You should learn to be proud of your accomplishments," Mr. Marshall said. Mr. Marshall is a banker and I could see how he was proud about everything in his life, including Bobby.

Bobby didn't buy it. "I am proud of them. I just don't like to brag about things."

"Who's bragging?" Mr. Marshall turned to me. "RV, am I bragging?"

"RV, don't answer that," Mrs. Marshall interrupted before I could say anything. "Don't let George put you on the spot."

"Okay, okay. I get the hint," Mr. Marshall said, shaking his head. "RV, don't mind me. I get carried away with myself sometimes. Luckily, these two people keep me in line."

Mr. Marshall leaned over and held Mrs. Marshall's hand. Mrs. Marshall smiled back at him. Bobby seemed a little embarrassed, but then he relaxed when we began talking about other things.

Going home I couldn't help but feel a little jealous, comparing the dinner I had at Bobby's house with the dinners at our house. Sure, maybe they were on their best behavior because a guest was there. And, sure, maybe Bobby's dad annoyed him occasionally like all fathers do. But everyone really seemed to like one another. Not like my house. Or even Carole's house for that matter. That was big and upscale too. But it seemed so cold and empty compared to Bobby's. It was nice to know a happy family in my life, even though it makes me even sadder about my own.

Chapter Twelve

Guilt and Hope

I better remember to pray before going to bed tonight. For once it's not about looking at guys, ha ha. It's about Mr. Aniso. I feel bad at the way I've been treating him, and I could use some forgiveness. (There's the old guilt again. I wonder what Dostoyevsky would say about me.)

I shouldn't really feel that guilt because I'm doing what the other kids do, though that's not a good reason, is it? And I've been doing more of it, haven't I? Come on, RV, admit it. You've been giving Mr. Aniso a pretty hard time, haven't you?

Well, yes. But doesn't he deserve it? He's been a little too nice to me, and if I let him continue, I think he'd make me his pet. Oh, man, Aniso's pet! Gross! Horrible! Disgusting!

Yeah, I've been getting good grades in Latin, and I can conjugate and decline better than anybody, but that's because I have a head start. The mother tongue works the same way. So I don't deserve any praise for that since I didn't ask to be born a Lith. I didn't ask to be born a lot of other ways too.

But I guess Mr. Aniso thinks differently. One time he said something about my exemplary homework to the class. Exemplary homework! No wonder people draw pictures of me with a halo. And then another time he handed out a quiz and said something about how everyone else should study as hard as I do and get good grades.

Thanks a lot, Mr. Aniso. When he mentioned studying hard, I saw Duffy and Doyle exchange glances.

That's what worries me the most. What if I'm giving out some kind of gay vibe and Aniso's picking up on it? And what if the other kids start picking up on it too? Then I'm really dead meat. I might as well just get ready for Duffy and Doyle to corner me in the locker room.

I've been fighting back though. Lately, I've been making fun of Aniso as much as everyone else, maybe even more. I've made some good limp wrist motions after he walks by me in class. And I'm even the one who came up with the nickname we now use for him. Gaius Anus. Even Duffy and Doyle like that one. "Hey, Gaius! How's your anus?" Duffy yelled once when a group of us kids were leaving after school, and we saw Mr. Aniso leaving too.

He didn't hear it. Or pretended not to. And I laughed with the other kids who were there. At least it keeps me from being cornered in the locker room. So far, anyway.

But I don't really feel good about it. The other day Mr. Aniso was handing back another homework assignment. And when he gave me mine, he paused and gave me this look. I don't know. There was something in his eyes, Something very sad. And it really shook me up.

Maybe I'm just imagining it. Maybe it's my own guilt talking. After all, guilt can do crazy things as the guy in *Crime and Punishment* found out.

Oh, man. Now I wish I'd never read the book. It's like the guy was writing about my life. And I don't like what I see about my life sometimes. And worse, sometimes what I don't like most of all is myself.

*

At least I like my crazy family more these days. The layoffs are over, and the situation at Dad's work has leveled off, so he's not quite as freaked out about money as before. Though I know he'll never stop worrying about it totally. Ray has settled down a bit too. He and Dad did go to see Sister Hell Dog, and I was dreading what would happen. But Ray didn't get suspended, and Dad didn't beat the crap out of him when they got home. They never told us what was said in Sister Hell Dog's office. Ray must have convinced them of his innocence. Who knows? Perhaps he really is innocent, and I'm not being fair to him. Wouldn't be the first time in life someone is not being treated fairly, right?

Dad and Ray appear to have made some kind of pact to try to not drive each other crazy. Okay, I hope so. When they drive each other crazy, they drive me crazy too.

Best of all, though, has been Mom. Her online jewelry business has started bringing in a little extra cash, and today at dinner she told us another piece of good news. Through a contact she made online, she has a chance to sell her jewelry in a small store in downtown Boston.

"What's the downside?" Ray asked, speaking English of course.

"Downside?" I explained to Mom what that meant, giving Ray a dirty look. For all his complaining about Dad, here he was doing the same thing, focusing on something negative right off the bat. I guess you can never expect a complete turnaround in a person.

But Mom didn't see any downsides. The owner of the shop promised to sell Mom's jewelry on consignment, if she helped out in the store two evenings a week. Mom was happy because it wouldn't interfere with her part-time day job at Nieman Marcus and she could still do her online business.

Dad didn't seem all that pleased. "*Consignment? Kas tas consignment*?" he asked, frowning a little, wanting to know what consignment meant.

Mom explained the store would show her jewelry to customers and pay her when one of her pieces of jewelry was sold. But any pieces of jewelry that were not sold were hers to keep.

"Consignment. Consignment." Mom repeated the word a couple of times, looking like she enjoyed the sound of it.

Dad was more interested in exactly how much they would pay her.

Mom said she would get two-thirds of the money and the store would keep a third. She told us that was a good rate, which she got in exchange for agreeing to work at the store two evenings a week.

Dad didn't seem convinced but he didn't say anything for once. Mom seemed so happy, I didn't want to say anything to upset her either. But Mom already seems stressed out with trying to sell the jewelry from home and juggling that with her job at Neiman Marcus. Won't this be even more work? Mom doesn't think so, but I'm not so sure.

I didn't say anything to Mom though. I can't get into the negative space where Dad and Ray go so often. It was nice to see Mom in such a good mood. It's good to see someone in this family happy and hopeful for a change.

*

And something else positive!

I've been hanging out with Bobby Marshall more and more. I still can't really believe Bobby is spending time with me. He's no goof-off in class, he's on every team I can think of, and all the girls want to date him. I still don't get it. Sure I'm better at English than he is, and I'm helping him to write better papers, but is that why he wants to be friends?

I wish I didn't feel so cynical about it. That's another pretty cool word that's been popping up all over the place. Cynical. It means you don't believe anything anyone says because everyone has a secret agenda or is lying. Hello! Who doesn't lie in life? Some people have to lie because it's their profession, like spies. And politicians, ha ha. But what about regular people, people like me? Don't we lie? I guess we do sometimes. But does that mean we have to be cynical too? Through all of life? Is that another one of your tricks, oh Big Guy?

I'm seeing Bobby tomorrow at Joe's to help him with a history paper. Maybe there's a way I find out what he really thinks of me. I can't really ask him directly, can I? Maybe I can test him some way. That's terrible. There I go being cynical. Didn't I just promise myself not to go to that negative place? Instead, I'm going from being hopeless to turning cynical. What a combo, a b-a-a-a-d combo.

*

"*Pakviesk Bobby pietums.*" Mom suggested. "Invite Bobby to dinner."

"*Į mūsų namus? Čia??*" "To our house? Here?"

"*Taip. Kodėl ne?*" "Yes. Why not?" Dad chimed in.

I had been telling them about Bobby and what a great time I had at his house. Mistake. So now Mom and Dad want me to return the favor and invite him here. I guess they're curious about my new friend too. They have met Carole, so why not Bobby? Have I really been talking about him that much? It's a parent's right to be curious, I suppose. I couldn't argue with that. But dinner here? With my crazy family?

I hesitated.

Dad asked me what was wrong.

"Nothing's wrong," I wanted to say. "But can I trust my new friend with you guys? Do you promise to behave and not fight?" Of course I didn't say that and just shrugged. I asked them if they were sure, stalling for time. They both nodded. And that's how I ended up inviting Bobby to dinner.

When the doorbell rang, I sent up a special prayer to the Big Guy. "Okay, Big Guy. If I ever needed you, it's now. Please, please, don't let my parents screw this up for me. If they don't, I'll owe you big time." At least there was one thing good. Ray had gotten out of the dinner, so he wasn't around. One less thing to worry about.

Mom opened the front door, and there was Bobby, smiling and looking so nice, dressed in slacks and an open-collar shirt. He was holding a bunch of red roses. "These are for you," he said. "RV told me how much you like roses." He held them out to her.

"Oh, thank you so much," Mom said, taking the roses. She smiled her most polite smile.

And then it hit me. Bobby is black, and I never told Mom and Dad. I didn't feel I needed to because I hardly notice it myself. I mean, what's the big deal? Bobby is a person. But I know a lot of people still do notice these things. And Mom and Dad have said some racist things in the past.

Do I think a lot of Liths are racist? When I confronted Mom and Dad once, they defended themselves. They said they weren't racist. They said all those East European countries were occupied by so many other horrible regimes, like the German Nazis and the Russian communists, they were just sick of outsiders and wanted to be left alone.

"So anyone black or Muslim is an outsider?" Ray had asked.

They shrugged, ignoring the question, but I'm sure the answer was yes.

So here I was, letting an outsider into our house, without even thinking about it.

"Please, please, Big Guy," I prayed again, as Bobby walked into the living room and shook hands with Dad. "Please, Big Guy. I didn't think about this part. If Mom and Dad don't say anything stupid, I'll go to church every day for a month. And I'll put a third, no half, of my allowance in the collection basket."

I took a breath as we all sat down in the living room. Mom and Dad tried to smile, though I could see a lot of things were going on in their minds.

"So, RV tells me you are sportsman. Good sportsman," Dad said in his wonderful English.

Bobby shrugged. "Thanks. I try."

"You play basketball?" Dad continued. "Lithuania. Good basketball players there. *Krepšinis,* our sport. National sport. We win in Olympics. I try to help RV appreciate, but no. He have no interest."

"Well," Bobby said. "Not everybody can like the same things. RV is great in English and other languages too. He helps me write better papers."

"Bobby, would you like something to drink while we're waiting for dinner?" Mom said in her most polite voice. "We have Coca-Cola, ginger ale, lemonade."

"I offer this," Dad said, chuckling and holding out his glass. "Our national sport too. Vodka. You wait a few years. Then I teach you about vodka. Good vodka. Better than Russian."

I started to cringe, Dad trying to make a joke. But Bobby laughed. "Thanks," he said to Dad, and then turned to Mom. "I'll have a Coke, please."

I asked for one, too, and Mom went into the kitchen to get us the Cokes. I desperately tried to think of another conversation starter, but Bobby came to my rescue.

"So, Mr. A.," he said. Then he shook his head, looking embarrassed. "I'm sorry. I have a hard time pronouncing your last name. As I said, I'm not good with languages."

Dad waved him off. "Okay. No problem. Most Americans shake heads when they see my last name."

I was afraid he'd get on his anti-American tirade, but Bobby asked him about his job after Mom came back with our Cokes. So thank God, he didn't go there. Instead, he started talking about his duties at work, feeling pressure to keep his job, and the layoffs. Bobby seemed genuinely interested, asking him more questions. Dad was glad to answer.

It made me realize Dad and I never talked about his job. It just never came up. Why? Did I not care? Did Dad want me to care?

Finally Mom, who had been going back and forth to the kitchen, announced that dinner was ready. We went to the table. Mom had made a big roast with potatoes and vegetables. There were a few awkward pauses and semi-embarrassing questions, but no stupid comments or opinions about white and black people that I had heard

Mom and Dad make in private. As delicious as the roast was, I could hardly eat a thing, expecting something embarrassing to be said at any moment or a stupid joke to be cracked, especially by Dad. But no. They were avoiding the race issue like it was poison, which I guess it would have been. There were enough touchy issues swirling around just below the surface without race adding to the mess.

We had some ice cream for dessert, and then it was finally time for Bobby to leave. I said a little prayer again, as he shook Dad's hand and Mom gave him a gentle pat on the shoulder, telling him to come back soon. I thanked the Big Guy for getting us through this without any huge disaster. But I did ask if I could take back my promise and contribute only a third of my allowance in church instead of half. I reminded Him about Dad's vodka comment and the indigestion I know I'll have for days.

*

I met Bobby at Joe's today. He told me he had a good time at dinner and thought my parents were nice.

I love it when friends say your parents are nice. Because they always do seem nice in front of other people. It's just that when you get home with them, you see who they really are.

I told Bobby as much.

"Don't be so sure everything is so hunky-dory at my house," he said, giving me a strange look. "We have our problems. We just know how to hide them in front of company."

"You mean like you father bragging? Almost like he was trying to prove how good you were? I picked up on that."

"Yes, that's part of it. Dad always wants us to be the best—in everything," Bobby added, looking unhappy. "He's got a chip on his shoulder about being black."

"What do you mean?"

"It's so important for him to show how good black people can be, how smart, how accomplished like him. He can't stand for any black person to be less than great or make a mistake." Bobby was getting animated. "It's almost like reverse racism," he said. "Prove to the White Man how good we are. But why do we have to prove anything? We are who we are!"

He suddenly stopped talking.

"I'm sorry," he said, turning to me and shaking his head. "Dad is putting a lot of pressure on me to do all these things, and it gets to me."

I wasn't sure what to say, so I just said, "I understand," trying to be supportive.

"Do you? Do you really understand, RV? You're white and you never had to deal with racism." Bobby looked almost angry.

"No, I haven't," I was forced to agree. But I felt a need to defend myself. "But I've had to deal with other things. Being a kid of immigrants is no picnic either."

"No, it isn't," Bobby agreed. Then he suddenly laughed. "Listen to us. Woe is me! My lot in life is worse than yours!"

I was glad to see him in a better mood.

"I'm sorry I got off on my high horse," Bobby said. "I didn't mean to take my frustration out on you."

"Hey, we all have our moments," I said, laughing, just to show there were no hard feelings. "You're right. We're doing okay and we should be happy about that."

Bobby nodded. "Yeah."

I meant what I said, though Bobby couldn't possibly understand how really happy I was. Having a heart-to-heart with Bobby and enjoying some good pizza at Joe's. Life really was good, wasn't it?

We talked some more about the pressure fathers put on sons. I told him a little bit about how my Dad was unhappy with a lot of things, how he couldn't seem to get used to this country, and to how I was sure he felt I didn't measure up to the son he wanted to have.

"Sometimes I wonder if I try hard enough to make him happy," I said, shrugging. "But it just seems so difficult sometimes."

"I'm learning no matter how hard you try it's never good enough," Bobby said.

A bunch of other customers came in at that moment, crowding in around us.

Bobby suggested we continue our conversation elsewhere. "Let's take a walk."

We started walking, and Bobby told me a little more about how his father put pressure on him to win every game. "He says it's okay to lose, but that's only lip service. I see what his face looks like when we do lose or I screw up a play. It's making me want to quit the teams altogether."

"But you can't do that!" I said. "You're one of the best players the school has!"

"Now you're putting pressure on me."

"Sorry," I said, but Bobby was smiling.

"It's okay, RV. I appreciate the compliment."

We started walking through the woods near the ballpark and ended up near the same spot by the stream I visit with Carole.

"I enjoy the woods. Life is so peaceful and quiet here," Bobby said sitting down by the stream.

"Yeah. I enjoy the woods too," I said, sitting beside him. I felt a little guilty. This was my spot with Carole. Was it okay that I was now sitting here with Bobby?

"Do you come here a lot?" I asked Bobby.

"Sometimes. When I need time to think after practice."

"Yeah, I come here too. But I've never seen you here." I told him about coming to this spot with Carole, feeling a need to confess it for some reason. I didn't tell him about making out with her up here though.

He nodded. "Yeah. It's a nice place." Then he grew quiet again, looking off into the distance.

"What are you thinking about?" I asked after a while.

"Oh, I'm just thinking about school, sorry." Bobby turned to me and smiled. "I have another project due for Latin class, but I didn't want to bother you with it. I feel like I've already taken enough advantage of you."

"Oh, I don't mind," I said.

Bobby smiled again. "Thanks. I appreciate it." Then he put his hand around my shoulders, gave them a little tug, and drew me closer. He held me there for a few seconds. "You're a good friend, RV."

I nearly jumped out of my skin. Having Bobby touch me was like a jolt of electricity going through my body. I've never felt anything like it before. From a simple touch.

It must have shown on my face because Bobby asked, "What's the matter?"

"Oh, ah, nothing," I stammered. "What's your Latin project on?" I asked, trying to change the subject.

"I'm trying to write a little a story about the Romans and have to use some words in Latin." He shook his head. "I don't know what Aniso was thinking. Can you imagine? Me writing a story? And with words in Latin? I wish I was in your class. It doesn't sound like Aniso gives you guys crazy assignments like that."

I laughed. "Don't be so sure. Our assignments are no picnic either."

Bobby was in another one of Mr. Aniso's classes. I felt myself tense up, waiting for the usual jokes about Mr. Aniso.

But Bobby didn't go there. Instead he asked, "Do the kids in your class make fun of him?"

I nodded. My mouth was feeling dry. I didn't want to tell him I did my share of making fun of Mr. Aniso too.

"It must be hard for him," Bobby said after a while. "Being gay and all. It's like he's fighting for himself all the time." The look on Bobby's face was the same sad one I thought I saw on Mr. Aniso's face the time he gave my paper back to me.

I didn't know what to say. What was Bobby trying to tell me? That he wasn't one of those people who didn't make fun of gay people? That he wouldn't make fun of me if he thought I was gay? And why was he so sad? I wanted to give him a hug to comfort him, but of course I didn't dare.

We sat there for a while looking out into the distance to the hills. It's funny how with some people you can be together without saying anything and still feel so connected with them. You don't have to say anything because whatever you say won't mean more than what you're feeling already.

That's how I felt sitting there with Bobby. And I didn't want to move, wanting to sit there and feel connected with him forever.

Chapter Thirteen

Imagination and Reality

It hit me like a ton of bricks as I was going to bed last night. Could Bobby be gay? I can't believe I'm saying it, but that's the thought that popped into my head. I mean there's nothing gay about Bobby. Like I've said before, he's all guy. But, but there I go. I'm stereotyping, aren't I? You don't have to be like McGrath or Mr. Aniso to be gay, right?

And what about me? I might not be the most macho guy in class (ha!), but I'm not a flamer, right? I mean, Duffy and Doyle haven't picked on me yet—not for that, anyway. And no one else has said anything. Okay, I'm supposed to be an angel (like I keep saying, if they only knew!), but that's not really gay, is it? Angels are straight, ha ha.

So why can't Bobby be gay? It's not like I'm saying he's an alien or anything. It's not impossible he could be gay, right? He's friendly with a lot of girls, but he's friendly with everybody, guys and girls. And I don't hear anything about him dating anyone. Even Cynthia Hoevermeyer, the stuck-up bimbette in English class who thinks she's Miss America and has been after Bobby since the first day of school.

(Bimbette—that's my word. If I only had the balls to call Cynthia bimbette to her face. "Hi, Bimbette." "Did you get another hundred on the quiz, Bimbette?" "Who you taking to the prom, Miss Bimbette?" *Crapola*! I just Googled "bimbette" and it's already there. Been around for a long time, I guess. Oh, well. Better luck next time, RV.)

Anyway, I've got to calm down. Bobby *might* be gay. I didn't say Bobby *was* gay. And what am I basing my assumption on? That he didn't make fun of Mr. Aniso? So, a lot of people don't make fun of Mr. Aniso. But Bobby's a jock, and most jocks make fun of him. So? What does that prove? Just that he's even a nicer guy than I thought.

What about when Bobby and I were sitting together in the woods yesterday? When I felt so connected to him? That meant something, right? But what? And how do I know Bobby felt the same thing?

Then why did he hug me like that? Okay, okay, it wasn't really a hug. Just a friendly arm on my shoulders. But he did draw me closer to himself. So? Why am I reading so much into that? It doesn't have to mean anything.

I guess I'm letting my fantasies get the better of me. Who would think a simple friendly gesture would feel so...so major. But it was. I've never felt like that before. It's as if my whole body came alive. That's a stupid thing to say, isn't it? My body's been alive for fourteen years. But this felt different. Like everything changed in an instant. Like all my feelings suddenly connected together in some deep way.

Okay, RV. Calm down! Put Bobby out of your mind! Put being gay out of your mind. There's no proof of anything. You're letting your imagination go wild. Call Carole and ask her to put on one of her new bras for you. And get to your homework. You've got your own project for Mr. Aniso to finish.

*

Mom and Dad are at it again. It turns out Mom needs some extra money to get her share of the space to sell jewelry at the store downtown—$2,500 to be exact. Kind of like a down payment, I guess. Of course Mom doesn't have that kind of money lying around, so today at dinner she told Dad she would have to borrow it from the family savings account. Mom and Dad have been putting money into that account for as long as I can remember. They're hoping to get a bigger house someday.

And you can just imagine what Dad said. He reminded her what the money was for.

She reminded him they were both putting money into that account.

He asked her what would happen if her business went bust.

She told him she would work hard to make sure it didn't go bust.

He told her there were no guarantees in business.

And so it went. Pretty soon they were calling each other worse names than negative or not realistic. Mom started talking about a divorce. When Mom gets really angry, she comes right out and says she wants to leave Dad. That makes Dad angrier than anything. Usually at that point Mom drops the subject and no one takes her seriously.

But today she seemed as angry as Dad. She just got up and left the table without finishing her food.

Ray and I sat there, trying to keep eating. Dad sat there without saying anything. He wasn't eating either. Finally, he turned to me.

"*Nu. Ko žiūri taip į mane?*" "Why are you looking at me like that?"

If I was looking at Dad in any particular way, I wasn't aware of it. "Don't take your anger out on me," I wanted to say. But of course I didn't say anything. If he was feeling guilty about yet another argument with Mom, that was his problem, not mine.

Dad looked away from me and to Ray, who didn't have his phone with him for once. "What?" Ray said, shrugging.

But Dad just frowned and looked down at his food. He didn't start eating. He didn't do anything. He just kept frowning.

I couldn't eat anymore, either, and I wanted to leave the table. I could tell Ray felt the same way. When everyone is stewing in their own thoughts but still pretending to be a family, it's torture. Why pretend?

I stood up to go, but Dad slapped the palm of his hand on the table and told me to finish my food. I told him I wasn't hungry, but he didn't want to listen. Maybe that's what gets me maddest of all. He's the biggest one for pretending.

"Well, I'm finished," Ray said, and he stood up to go. His plate looked clean, but I saw he had taken the rest of his food, put it into his napkin, and hid the napkin under the table. It was in his hand when he stood up.

He left before Dad could say anything. So I had to sit there, alone with Dad, trying to force down the rest of my meal.

Another wonderful family dinner. And now no one's talking to one another. And it will be like that for a while. Then someone will say something and we'll all start talking again. And maybe even Dad will break down and stop giving Mom grief about the money.

I'm getting used to this pattern. But it doesn't mean I like it any better. I'm reading *The Godfather* now, and I'm feeling more and more that my family is like the family in the book, the Corleones. But instead of killing other families we're killing one another. While pretending not to. It would almost be better if I woke up with a dead horse in my bed some morning, like it happens to that guy in the book.

*

The Big Guy really punched me in the stomach this time. Landed one right in my gut. Pow!

I was going to Joe's Pizza this afternoon, but who did I see coming out but Bobby, with a girl. And not just any girl. Miss Bimbette herself, Cynthia Hoevermeyer.

Bobby and Cynthia Hoevermeyer? Just when I had convinced myself Bobby wasn't dating any girls.

I hid behind a tree and let them pass. They certainly looked like they were doing more than just sharing pizza. They were both laughing, and after Bobby said something Cynthia threw her arms around his shoulders in that cutesy way she does with guys she goes out with.

But how did this happen? And when? Bobby hasn't said anything to me about dating Cynthia. Not that he has to. But I thought we were friends. I guess not as good friends as I thought. Cynthia's not the type to keep something like this quiet, though, so it must have happened pretty recently. I thought she was going out with the hockey team captain, but obviously they've broken up.

I've been trying to push it out of my mind. So, Bobby's going out with Cynthia Hoevermeyer. Why should I care? If he really likes her and didn't say anything to me that says something about him. And it's a good lesson for me about letting my fantasies get out of hand.

Easier said than done. I came home after seeing Bobby and Cynthia, trying to forget all about it. But when I went to sleep I had another weird dream. I dreamed Bobby invited me to shoot hoops again. Without thinking why in the world he would, I accepted. But when I went to his house, who was there with him but Duffy and Doyle. They forced me to keep shooting baskets, and every time I missed, each one took a turn throwing me against some lockers. Bobby stood and watched, not doing anything to stop them. Then Cynthia came out of Bobby's house with a tray of lemonade. She offered each of us a glass, even me. But when I started drinking my glass I realized it was milk, kind of lukewarm and disgusting the way my father likes it. I wanted to complain but I didn't dare because they were looking at my every move.

Not a feel-good dream. But then real life doesn't feel good either.

*

Okay, Big Guy. It's late at night and I can't sleep. I've been crying. Isn't that stupid? But I can't help it. It's not really about Bobby and Cynthia Hoevermeyer, though it's about that too. It's more about how stupid I've been to let my imagination go wild and start getting all worked up over Bobby. Imagining things I had no right imagining. A good lesson about life.

It's the best one you've given me so far, Big Guy. Not just one punch in the gut. More like a total knockdown. Thank you very much. So what am I supposed to learn from this one? You can't count on things turning out the way you want them to? It's easy to fool yourself? You can't trust anyone, most of all yourself?

That's all pretty cynical, isn't it? Maybe that's the real lesson. There are times in life when it's better to be cynical. Being cynical gets you through life so you don't get hurt or go totally insane.

Chapter Fourteen

Merry-go-round

Something happened to Mr. Aniso. A substitute teacher was there to greet us in Latin class today. She told us Mr. Aniso got hurt over the weekend and was in the hospital. She didn't give us any other details. We got an official notice not giving much more information and just wishing him a speedy recovery. But there were a lot of rumors flying around. Some kids said what we were told wasn't the whole story. They heard some guys caught him coming out of a bar late on Saturday night and beat him up. Other kids even said the guys were friends of Duffy and Doyle.

I feel bad. I was starting to like Mr. Aniso. He's a good teacher. Hard on us, but fair. And he doesn't take any crap from anyone, even Duffy and Doyle. What if the rumor about his getting beat up is true, and Duffy and Doyle are behind what happened to him? That's really scary.

At least I stopped making fun of Mr. Aniso, so my conscience is okay on that score. But I still feel bad for the times I did make fun of him before. Now I wish I hadn't. But you can't take things back, especially mean things.

Mr. Aniso's replacement tried hard today but I don't know how she'll do. Her name is Miss Carlson, but we've already given her a nickname: the Milkmaid. That's because she has really light skin, like milk, and she wears her hair in two long braids. She looks as if she's from a farm in Vermont or something. And she's real serious. Never smiles.

Whalen, the guy who called me an angel, came up with her nickname. He even drew a picture of her trying to milk a cow. It was funny. The guy has talent, though I'm not exactly sure for what.

Oh, well. Maybe the Milkmaid will loosen up. We'll just have to put up with her until she does. There are more important things to worry about at school. Like not making a fool of myself again with Bobby Marshall.

Sitting next to him in Biology is really hard these days. Bobby's still friendly, but different too. Like he knows I know about him and Cynthia, even though we haven't talked about it. But Bobby and Cynthia aren't trying to hide it. Now I see them walking together in the hallways and leaving school together after classes. I don't feel like it's my place to ask Bobby about Cynthia, since he never mentioned anything to me. So we don't go there. But it's there anyway, unspoken, hovering around us like some weird ghost.

It gets me frustrated, though, because I still think about Bobby. And the dreams don't stop. Last night I dreamed we were running together in a field of yellow flowers, the way they do in those lovey-dovey perfume commercials. Another time I dreamed we were holding hands skydiving.

I think those are gay dreams. I can't deny that, can I? But what do the dreams mean? In one book I read about the founders of modern psychology, Freud and Jung. They talked about dreams a lot. But they lived a hundred years ago. Things have changed. They didn't even have the internet then, not to mention a lot of other things. So maybe dreams don't mean what they used to. Or maybe they do. All these questions. These days my mind is like a merry-go-round of thoughts that just keep spinning around but don't go anywhere. I wish there was someone to talk to.

Home is a merry-go-round too. Of crap. Ray is still in a world of his own, even though we haven't gotten any more calls from Sister Hell Dog. It's like he's not even part of this family.

At least Mom and Dad haven't bothered me too much about Bobby. They both said how nice he was, as if I needed confirmation of the fact. No comments about his being black either. I sometimes think they want to say something about it, but they're not sure what. It's like they want to be PC and all that, but they're not sure how being PC works. Because they're not really PC down deep. But I guess they're trying, so I should give them some credit for that.

Maybe they're not thinking too much about Bobby because all their energies are still about being mad at each other. Dad is still annoyed at Mom for taking $2500 from our savings account for her jewelry business. And he's sniping about it, saying what a risky business it is and is she sure she knows what she's doing. Mom, in turn, is annoyed with him, saying he should be more understanding and supportive. She tells him they won't get anywhere in this country without trying something new.

At least they haven't said anything more about a divorce, so things are the same as always as far as that goes. Is that good or bad? I don't know anymore.

And there's more Lith stuff going on too. Christmas was bad enough, but February and March are also pretty bad. February 16 is Lithuanian Independence Day, when

Lithuania declared independence in 1918, when World War I ended. But there's another Independence Day marking March 11, 1990, when Lithuania declared independence from the Soviet Union, which had occupied the country after World War II. All these independence days! I guess when you're a small, pissant country no one cares about, you have to keep declaring independence, hoping one of those times it will stick. I'd like to have a few of those too.

To commemorate all those independence days, Liths have *minėjimai,* where we have to go to the Lith Club in Boston and listen to boring speeches. And then there's usually a cultural part to the proceedings, of course. Maybe a fat opera singer from Lithuania or a guy with greasy hair playing the violin. Dad used to be on the planning committees for these things, so in previous years we not only had to go to these functions, we had to do a volunteer bit for them too. Luckily this year, Dad had a fight with one of the planning committee guys, so we got out of the planning part.

And there's another function, *Kaziuko Mugė*, which is also in March. I don't know how to translate that exactly. It's another tradition thing, named after St. Casimir, who was the patron saint of Lithuania and Poland, which were one country in the Middle Ages. (By the way, Casimir's name in Lithuanian was *Kazimieras,* which is my confirmation name. Arvydas Kazimieras Aleksandravičius. And you thought that Arvydas Aleksandravičius was hard to say!)

St. Casimir was a real holy guy, as they keep reminding us. His family ruled the two countries, but Casimir found time to pray and do a lot of good deeds while he was ruling. He never married either because they say he was so chaste. So instead of thinking about girls he must have spent time doing crafts because *Kaziuko Mugė* is a big crafts fair. It takes place early in March, which is when he died.

Dad is on the planning committee for that now, and he's spending a *lot* of time with preparations. And guess who he has helping him. Yup, yours truly. In past years Mom's been in on the action, too, and baked some cakes for the fair. But this year she's so busy with her new business she probably won't bake anything. Besides, she's still mad at Dad.

She told Dad the other day to be careful and not overdo his volunteering for St. Casimir's Day, so that he doesn't forget the needs of his family. Dad took her comment as an insult, of course. So more arguing. These days it seems there's so little they can agree on. I wish I could tell Dad to cut down on the volunteering, too, or at least leave me out of it. But I know how important it is to him and how upset he'd be if I said something.

I'd like to talk to Bobby about it, about all that pressure, since he's got pressure of his own. But something's changed since that day in the woods when we felt so close. He's got Cynthia now and our closeness feels different. I don't know how else to describe it. I wish I could put my finger on it.

That reminds me. I learned a great new word! It's *schadenfreude*. It's pronounced *shade* but with an *ah*, like when you stick your tongue out. *Schahhd*. Then *in Freud*, like good ol' Sigmund's name. And then a quick *eh* at the end, sort of like little old ladies ask when they can't hear what you said and put their hands to their ears. *Eh? Eh? Schahhd-in-Freud-eh*. It's German, and it means you're happy when things go wrong for other people. I don't want *schadenfreude* for Bobby, of course. Maybe for Cynthia.

Oh, that's terrible. But I have to be honest, I'm upset. And a little jealous. I have to admit it. So, yes, a little *schadenfreude* for Cynthia. Okay. So I can't be chaste and holy like St. Casimir. But I don't think I'm so bad either. Maybe I'll get over being jealous at some point. If there is a heaven, I wonder if there's room for people in the middle like me.

*

"Mom and Dad are getting a divorce."

Boy, the bad news is coming from all quarters. That was Carole today. I haven't seen her in ages, and I was glad she called. We were sitting on her sofa, and I was feeling a little uncomfortable. I know I'm partly to blame for not calling her, but then she hasn't called either. So what's up with that?

Carole was sitting in the corner of the sofa, scrunching up her legs against her chest and holding them tightly. Her eyes looked puffy, like she'd been crying, and her hair was stringy, like she didn't wash it this morning.

"My parents are getting a divorce," she repeated.

"Oh, I'm sorry."

Carole shrugged. "I don't know why I'm so shocked. I've told you before how they're hardly together, so why should I be surprised?"

"Are you sure it's definite?" I asked, trying to find something good to say.

"I think so." Carole nodded slowly. "Last night they sounded like they really mean business."

"I'm sorry," I repeated stupidly. What else was there to say?

Carole didn't say anything. She kept staring straight ahead, sitting in the corner of the sofa with her arms around her legs, like a little ball you could just roll around on the floor. I felt bad for her. I had never seen her quite so down.

Then big tears started going down her cheeks. She wasn't even sobbing or doing anything else to show she was crying. She sat there like a stone, not saying anything, staring straight ahead. But the big tears kept coming, rolling down her cheeks one after another.

I couldn't stand it any longer. I moved up next to her and hugged her. She put her head down on my shoulder and hugged me back. We sat for a long time, quiet, lost in our own thoughts. What can you say at a time like that?

She finally looked up. "Thanks, RV. Thanks for coming over."

"Maybe things won't be so bad," I said, still trying to think of something positive to say.

She sat up against the sofa and wiped some tears from her cheeks with the back of her hand. "Don't bet on it. Mom's going to have a hard time alone. And she'll take it out on me."

"Maybe she'll meet someone."

"Yeah. Let's go sign her up with eHarmony. There will be guys lined up around the block."

"You sound like you don't mean it."

"Because I know Mom. She'll first have to get over feeling sorry for herself. And that will take a long time."

"And Dad?"

"Ha! Dad will be off doing whatever he's doing and we'll be lucky to get together once a year... If I'll want to." She turned her head away from me. "I don't know why some people have kids if they just think of them as a nuisance." She suddenly gazed up at me. "RV, are we still friends?"

"Of course. Why do you ask?"

She kept looking at me, almost like she was accusing me. "Well, I've hardly seen you lately. And when I do, you seem different."

"Different?"

"You're not going out with anyone else, are you?" We had never really talked about whether we were officially going out, we just did it. That's what I always loved about Carole. She was always so spontaneous, without making a big deal of things. Except now.

She asked me again if I was going out with anyone else, like she was impatient to know the answer.

"Of course not," I said, shaking my head. But as soon as the words were out of my mouth, an image of Bobby flashed through my mind. And then Bobby with Cynthia Hoevermeyer. "I don't want to go out with anyone else," I added for emphasis. I was hoping Carole wouldn't look up and see me blushing. "I—I've just had a lot on my mind."

"Like what?"

"Oh, just things."

I knew that was a nothing answer as soon as I said it. But I couldn't help it. How could I tell Carole everything that was on my mind?

Carole was quiet for a few moments, looking lost in thought. Then she moved closer to me and gave me a hug. "That's okay, RV," she said. "We all have a lot on our minds. I'm just glad you're here now."

I hugged her back. Whew! Another reason why I like her so much. She understands instinctively what I'm going through without my having to explain myself. It's a little scary, actually, but good. I have to promise myself I'll be careful in the future and not ignore her because I guess I have been doing that lately, at least a little.

Carole and I just held each other, hugging tightly. She was right. We hadn't done this in way too long. But something was still nagging at me, even as I was hugging her. Had something changed in my relationship with Carole?

The thought scared me. Too many things are changing in my life. Too fast. Bobby, Cynthia, Mom, Dad, school, and Mr. Aniso getting hurt. I don't know what to expect anymore. Or how I'm supposed to behave in all this confusion. Another good idea for an app, but I know that won't happen. I'll just have to stumble through it all, like I've been doing all along.

*

Well, we all survived the crafts fair dedicated to good old St. Casimir. Even Mom broke down and baked a small cake. There were a bunch of doohickeys and thingamajigs at the fair from Lithuania or made to look like they were. Dolls in national costumes. Crosses. Things made out of straw and wood: puppets, pipes, shoes, weird carvings of devils. Lithuanians love devils. Makes me wonder why. But there's religious stuff, too, to make up for it: plants for Palm Sunday, Easter eggs, and other food, like a cookie made from honey.

But since I'm not a crafts kind of guy and I didn't see the S-heads or anyone else I knew, I found a quiet place in the back of the hall and read my book. I finished *The Godfather* and have now started to read a new book called *Cancer Ward*. I showed the book to Carole when I got it from the library, and she said I was being morbid. It's about this Russian guy who has cancer and is stuck with other patients in a cancer ward. He eventually gets released but other people don't. The author, Alexander

Solzhenitsyn, was kind of cool. He had a long beard and he wrote the book when the communists were in charge of Russia. But he didn't like the communists, so he compared the country to a cancer ward. It's a metaphor. That's what I told Carole. She just looked at me strangely when I said that. Carole's more interested in her own problems than metaphors these days.

Maybe I should be more interested in how to solve my life than thinking about metaphors too. But books about that part of the world interest me. Is it my immigrant background coming out? I should be concentrating more on this country. The US is my present. Russia and Lithuania represent my past. Not just my past, but my family's past. I thought Mom and Dad had come here to shake off that past. I guess it's easier said than done.

Maybe that's why I like *Cancer Ward*. I feel stuck too. Stuck with my thoughts and feelings about Bobby and even Carole. They just keep popping up and going round and round in my head. And I can't move forward, no matter how hard I try to figure things out. I wonder if someday I'll get released or if I'm one of those unlucky stiffs who stays in the cancer ward.

Chapter Fifteen

Fear, Shame, and Anger

I went to see Mr. Aniso in the hospital today. We got an email from school telling us he was recovering well and he'd be happy for visitors. So I just had to go. He's at Brigham and Women's Hospital, which is not far from school, so I knew how to get there.

"It's the second room on the left," a nurse in a reception area told me after I found my way to the right floor.

Walking down the corridor to the room, I felt nervous. Would Mr. Aniso really be happy to see me? What would I say? And I suddenly remembered I hadn't brought anything like flowers or candy. Weren't you supposed to do that on a hospital visit?

Too late now. I walked into the room. Mr. Aniso was in bed. He was lying on top of the covers, watching TV. His head and his right arm were all bandaged up. When Mr. Aniso saw me he covered himself with a bedsheet, but I saw there were more bandages running up his side and on his leg. If he was doing better now, I'd hate to have seen him when he first got hurt.

"Hi." Mr. Aniso's voice sounded raspy and weak, not at all like the high-pitched but authoritative voice we made fun of in class.

"Hi, Mr. Aniso."

He regarded me like he was searching for something.

"It's RV from your Latin class."

"Yes, I know who you are." He coughed a little and turned his head, as if he was trying to make himself more comfortable. "Thank you for coming." He smiled weakly. "I'm just a little slow on the uptake these days."

"Yes, umm, they told us you wanted visitors, and I...and I wanted to come and..." My voice faded as Mr. Aniso coughed again. Why did I want to come? What was I supposed to say now I was here?

"I...I just wanted to come to show you my support and wish you a speedy recovery." There. That sounded good, right?

Mr. Aniso nodded slowly. Then he pointed to a chair by the foot of the bed. "RV, pull up a chair and make yourself comfortable."

"Oh, thanks." I put my jacket on the back of the chair and brought it over closer to Mr. Aniso. He watched me sit down.

I'd seen enough TV shows where people visited friends and family members in the hospital. Somehow they always seemed to know what to say to one another. Or else they just cried. I didn't know what to say. And I wasn't about to cry either, though I did feel pretty awful seeing Mr. Aniso lying there, all bandaged up.

Mr. Aniso pulled himself up a little bit so he was sitting a little higher against his pillow. "I'm sorry I'm a little out of it today, RV. I have good days and bad days."

I nodded.

"But I really do appreciate your coming."

I nodded again.

Mr. Aniso smiled a little. "How's Miss Carlson doing?"

"She's okay," I said, shrugging. "She's still trying to get a handle on the class."

"What do you mean?"

"Well, we kind of take advantage of her." I felt myself blushing and I knew I had to fess up. "She tries to give us homework, and we tell her it's too hard or we haven't gotten that far in the lesson plan yet. So she believes us and gives us easier homework."

Mr. Aniso smiled again, a little broader this time. "Not like me. You know you wouldn't get away with that with me around."

"How long—how long do you think it will be before you're back in class?" I blurted out.

"I don't know. Weeks, months. It depends on how quickly things heal. The most important thing is my head. I got a pretty deep gash in my skull when I...fell." He touched his head where the bandage was, as if to check whether it was still there and made a face.

"You fell?"

Mr. Aniso turned away from me and stared up to the ceiling. He stared for a long time. Then he turned back to me.

"Or else I was pushed. I'm not sure. There was so much confusion when they jumped me..."

"They?"

"Yes, they. I don't really know who they were. Some punks, I guess. It was too dark to see much." Mr. Aniso paused and looked up at the ceiling again, and then he turned back to me. "You see, I was coming out of a bar, which is on a small dark street. I heard some footsteps and some yelling. I heard the word 'faggot.'"

Mr. Aniso paused. I could tell he was gauging my reaction to what he was saying. Especially the word "faggot." I hoped I wasn't blushing or fidgeting. I was used to hearing some kids saying that, like when Duffy and Doyle picked on McGrath or other people. But hearing Mr. Aniso say it sounded worse somehow. More serious, like it meant something much more than just an insulting word.

"You see the bar I went to is a gay bar, so the punks know gay people come and go on that street. I went there for a drink and was on my way home."

Mr. Aniso looked at me again. I didn't know how to respond, so I just nodded.

Both of us looked at each other, not saying anything. Then Mr. Aniso asked me to hand him a plastic cup filled with water from the nightstand by his bed. He took a few sips through a straw and then asked me to put it back again.

He had slid down the bed and pulled himself back up again. "RV," he said, looking right at me. "I'm gay, in case you were wondering."

"Oh, okay." The way he said it, so matter of fact, so out there. It was good because it was so...so regular.

"Does it bother you?"

I shook my head,

"It bothers some people."

"Well, they're just ignoramuses." I didn't know where my anger came from, but suddenly I felt like taking on the whole world and paying it back for what they had done to Mr. Aniso.

"Ignoramuses or not, people like that can do a lot of damage." He motioned to himself. "As you can see in my case."

"I heard some kids say Duffy and Doyle are behind it."

Mr. Aniso shrugged. "Maybe. Maybe not. There are enough Duffys and Doyles in this world, so no one can say for sure. I certainly didn't see them or hear them."

"What—what are you going to do when you get back to class?" I wanted to know.

"Teach. What else am I supposed to do? That's what I know and love to do."

Mr. Aniso reached over with his good hand and gripped me by the shoulder. Gripped me hard. "Don't be afraid, RV. Don't be afraid for me. I'll be fine." He paused and took a breath. "But most of all don't be afraid for yourself. Ever. You'll do fine too."

I nodded, but didn't say anything. What did he mean by that? Could he tell what was going on in my life? All the questions I had about myself and everything else?

Mr. Aniso released his grip on my shoulder and lay back down on the bed. I sat like a stone, not moving, not knowing what else to say or do.

A nurse came in and told Mr. Aniso it was time for some medicine. I was glad for the excuse to stand up and say goodbye.

"I'll—I'll come back again," I said as I was putting on my coat.

Mr. Aniso smiled. "Thanks," he said. "I'd like that."

*

I couldn't go home after seeing Mr. Aniso. I went to Joe's Pizza instead, where I could think in peace and quiet. I ordered two slices of pepperoni and a Coke, and sat in the farthest booth in the back.

So Mr. Aniso told me he was gay. Just like that. It didn't surprise me. But just hearing him say it like it was no big deal was good. A little scary though. So out in the open, vulnerable, I guess.

I took a big gulp of Coke and thought more about what Mr. Aniso said when he held my shoulder. About not being scared. Did he say that because he thinks I might be gay? Is it so obvious? What about other people, like Duffy and Doyle? Images of McGrath being thrown against the lockers filled my head again, like they always do when I think about being gay.

I tried to forget everything and just eat my pizza, ashamed at how scared I was. There it was, plain as day. I was scared. Just because I might be gay. The anger I felt sitting by Mr. Aniso's hospital bed came rushing back too. That was crazy, wasn't it? Being scared. Why was so much of my life about being scared?

"Hi, RV."

I looked up. Bobby Marshall was standing there. "Oh hi, Bobby."

He smiled. "I always come here to think in peace and quiet where no one can find me, but you always beat me to it."

"Oh, sorry. I won't bother you," I blurted out, my thoughts still on Mr. Aniso.

"No, no, that's okay. I'm just kidding." Bobby started to sit down in my booth but then stopped and gave me a funny look. "But I won't bother you if you don't want me to. You have that leave-me-alone look. I know what that's like."

"No, no, it's fine. Have a seat."

"Are you sure?"

"Uh-huh. Sure."

"Okay. Let me get some pizza."

Bobby went over to the counter and ordered some pizza. Maybe for the first time ever I wasn't happy to see him and wanted to be alone to sort out my thoughts. Mr.

Aniso. Being gay. Being scared. Being angry. I didn't want Bobby to see me like this.

"What's the matter, RV?"

"Huh? Oh. Nothing. Sorry."

Bobby had sat down with his slice and was staring at me. "You really look upset. Are you sure you don't want me to leave you alone?"

"No, no it's okay." I tried to smile though I'm sure it came out looking stupid.

Bobby looked a little embarrassed, as if he didn't know what to say. "Is...is there anything...anything I can help you with?"

I shook my head. "No. I'm just in my own world, and I need to get out of it."

Bobby started eating his pizza. He seemed to be a little confused. I felt bad I wasn't telling him what was on my mind.

"I—I went to see Mr. Aniso in the hospital today, and I'm still thinking about it."

Bobby looked up." Oh, yeah. Poor guy. How did he look?"

"Pretty bad. His head is all bandaged up. He said he fell when he was jumped and hit his head pretty hard. He had bandages on his arm, too, and on one whole side down his leg."

"Does he know who jumped him?"

I shook my head. "He's not sure, but he thinks it was some punks out for some fag bashing." I took a breath and continued. "Mr. Aniso told me he was leaving a gay bar that night and the punks who beat up on him were calling him faggot." I glanced at Bobby's face. Tried to see if what I said had any effect on him. If he was at all uncomfortable, he covered it up pretty well.

"So he admitted he was gay?"

"Yes." Was that a statement on Bobby's part or an accusation?

"It's too bad there are still so many assholes in the world," Bobby said. His response made me feel a little better.

"Yeah, assholes is right," I agreed, my anger rising again.

"Did he say how long he would be in the hospital?" Bobby wanted to know.

I shook my head. "He's not sure."

Bobby thought for a while. "I guess we're stuck with the Milkmaid, maybe for the rest of the year."

I nodded and Bobby went back to his pizza. He looked like he was ready to stop talking about Mr. Aniso, so I stopped talking about him too.

We finished our pizza, not saying very much, and started walking back home. Bobby tried to joke with me and I tried to joke back with him, but I just couldn't get into it. Mr. Aniso was still on my mind.

"RV, what's the matter?" We had reached the ball field. Bobby had turned to look at me. "RV. I don't like to see a friend looking so down. I don't want to let you go home in this kind of mood."

I was touched that he still called me his friend. "I have a lot on my mind," I said.

"I can see."

Bobby suggested we go sit and talk some more before going home. So we went to the woods behind the field and sat on my favorite rock by the stream. It wasn't quite spring yet, but the late afternoon sun was strong, and it wasn't very cold. I stared over at the distant hills I always like looking at.

Bobby kept quiet, waiting for me to say something. And I just kept wondering if this was another joke the Big Guy was playing on me. A lot had happened in this place. Where I first kissed Carole. Where Bobby and I felt so close that one time. Would anything special happen this time?

"It's beautiful here, isn't it?" I said. "Being here calms me down."

Bobby nodded. "Yes, it's nice. I like being in nature too. We're both alike that way."

"Yeah, we are. Alike in a lot of ways except one," I wanted to say. A horrible thought occurred to me. "Do you bring Cynthia here?" I asked before I could stop myself.

Bobby gave me a strange look. "Oh yeah, Cynthia. I guess it's no secret."

"I'm sorry. It's none of my business," I said quickly. I could see talking about Cynthia was making Bobby uncomfortable. I was uncomfortable too.

He looked away and shrugged. "No, it's okay," he said. "So we're going out. What's the big deal?"

Yes, what was the big deal? For Bobby anyway.

He didn't look like he wanted to talk about Cynthia though. That was fine with me. I didn't want to talk about her either.

Bobby didn't say anything and then out of the blue he turned to me. "How do you know you really want to go out with someone?"

"Don't ask me. I'm no expert."

"But are you and Carole happy?"

I was kind of surprised by the question. "Well, yeah. I think so." So I guess everyone assumed Carole and I were going out. Maybe it was time I started assuming it too.

Bobby was quiet again, staring off into the distance. I wondered what he was thinking. Was he not happy with Cynthia? Is that what he was hinting at? I thought about Carole. I was happy with her, wasn't I? I had never really thought about it.

"What does being happy mean anyway?" I asked. "Sometimes I think I'll never be happy."

"Why do you say that?"

"Oh, I don't know," I lied. "Sometimes I think no matter how hard I try I'll never be able to figure myself out."

"I know what you mean."

"No you don't!" I wanted to shout. But I kept quiet, though the thought of Mr. Aniso in his hospital bed had me angry all over again.

"RV. Are you upset about Mr. Aniso?" Bobby asked finally.

I nodded.

"Look, he'll be okay. He told you himself, didn't he?"

"I know, I know. But I'm more upset about me than Mr. Aniso."

"You?"

"Yeah. I've been thinking a lot about myself, because well...because in some ways I'm like Mr. Aniso."

Bobby shook his head and even laughed. "You're nothing like Mr. Aniso."

"Well, in some ways, I am." If Bobby only knew.

"I don't think so."

"You don't know me that well." Why was I beating around the bush?

"Look, RV. Don't be so hard on yourself," Bobby said. "I'm hard on myself too. We're both hard on ourselves. Maybe that's why I like you so much."

Bobby seemed a little embarrassed after saying that. Though it made me feel good. But "Thanks" was about all I could manage to say in response, still getting all mushy inside whenever Bobby gave me a compliment.

Bobby became quiet again, gazing off into the distance. Suddenly he got up. "Oh, damn. Look at the time," he said, glancing at his watch. "I've got to be home for something."

I got up, too, and we started walking home.

"Well, good luck with Cynthia," I said, trying to make conversation.

"Yeah, thanks." And then he added, "And you. Good luck with not being hard on yourself."

"Yeah, thanks."

We walked the rest of the way not saying very much. Whenever I glanced over at Bobby, he seemed deep in thought, so I didn't want to disturb him.

I wondered what was on his mind. Maybe he was right. Maybe we both were hard on ourselves, just in different ways.

As for me, I couldn't believe how close I had come to blurting everything out about myself. It scared me. And it also made me mad. Why *didn't* I tell him everything that was on my mind? About sex and Carole and my gay thoughts and maybe even what I felt for him. That's what friends were for, weren't they? Was I just being a coward? I felt ashamed of myself again. Maybe it was about time to stop being cynical and trust people a little. Maybe it was time to trust myself a little.

*

Carole called me tonight. "Hey, RV, do you want to go to the movies with me and Tim?" she asked.

"Hmm, well, thanks but no thanks," I said after hesitating a little. "I'm kind of wiped tonight, so I think I'll stay in."

"But it's Saturday night." Good old Carole. Whenever she's down, she finds a way to pick herself up by doing something fun—and getting people around her to have fun too.

It took me a while, but I finally convinced her I really didn't want to go out, even if it was Saturday night.

"Okay, rest up. We'll miss you," she said. But she didn't sound too upset. I thought I actually heard her start giggling as she was hanging up the phone. I wondered if she was up to something, like planning to sneak into some new R-rated movie with Tim.

I have to admit I kind of wish I was with them. That way I could forget my life for a change. But on another level, I'm glad I said no. I just need to be alone. I'm still thinking of Mr. Aniso in the hospital bed. He looked so beat up. But not beaten down, if that makes sense. I went there to comfort him, but instead he ended up comforting me. That's pretty amazing. He really is different on the inside from what you'd expect he'd be like, given his swishiness outside. I'm starting to like him more and more. Even admire him. That's pretty amazing too.

*

I can't sleep. Well, I did fall asleep but then a nightmare woke me up. We were having dinner. Another one of our great family dinners where Mom and Dad were pretending everything was okay, not saying much of anything, and my brother was doing his usual thing, tuning it all out with his phone. Except at this dinner Mr. Aniso was there. He was sitting at the table next to me, chitchatting away with Mom and Dad like he was part of the family. But then everyone started squabbling and picking on Mr. Aniso. That made me mad, and instead of just shrinking into my chair, as usual, I stood up and told everyone to stop picking on him. They all looked at me surprised, and then they got angry. And then I woke up in a cold sweat.

I wish I knew what it all means. I'm glad I stood up to defend Mr. Aniso. At least I stood up for something, even if it was only in a dream. But why did I wake up in a cold sweat? I'm still scared, aren't I?

Chapter Sixteen

The Spring of My Discontent

It's spring. The sun is shining, the sky is blue, buds are appearing on the trees, everyone's out enjoying the warm rays—and I'm miserable. Oh, I shouldn't be so dramatic. But it's like in the Shakespeare play we read in English class, *Richard III*. Richard's brother is the king of England. Richard thinks he should be king. He's ugly and a hunchback. Not a good deal. So he calls it the winter of his discontent. Well, I may not be a hunchback, and I don't want to be a king, but I'm discontented too. For a lot of reasons.

I thought Bobby and I would get closer after our last talk, but he's still all over the place, friendly one minute and then cold the next, especially when Cynthia Hoevermeyer is around. Last week I was in Joe's Pizza when Bobby walked in—with Cynthia.

"Hi," he said, coming up to me.

"Hi, Bobby."

He seemed kind of uncomfortable. "You know Cynthia, right?"

"Hi, Cynthia."

"Hi."

We all just kind of looked at each other, not knowing what else to say.

"Well, enjoy your pizza, RV" was about all Bobby could manage.

"Yeah, enjoy yours."

They both walked away before I could decide whether to invite them to sit down or not. I wasn't so sure I wanted them to, and they probably weren't sure they wanted to sit with me anyway. They got their slices and sat in a booth on the other side of the room, pretty much as far away from me as you could get.

I tried not to look at them and acted nonchalant—boy, I never needed that word more than I did then. But I couldn't help sneaking a few peeks and saw Cynthia feeding Bobby part of her slice, putting a piece in his mouth like he was a four-year-old kid. I thought he gave me a look once or twice as if to say *get me outta here!*, but I'm sure that was my imagination because then he put part of his slice in her mouth. And they acted all kissy-pervy.

What's wrong with dufus me! Why can't I just stop paying attention to what Bobby's doing? He might call me his friend, but I'm not that important to him. That much is obvious. So why is he still so important to me?

Which reminds me, something's happening with Carole too. When's the last time she and I acted kissy-pervy like Bobby and Cynthia? The last few times we got together we still made out, but she didn't seem too into it. At first I thought she was upset about something, but Carole's not that kind of person. If she was upset, she would tell me. Maybe she wants to start exploring more than making out? I don't know if I'm ready for that.

The computer business has been kind of slow too. I hope she doesn't think it's my fault. I know I've been distracted a little with everything else going on in my life, but she's also been distracted, dealing with her parents' separation.

Maybe it's Tim. She's been hanging around with him more and more. Could she be getting a crush on him? That would be a surprise. His zits are getting worse, and he still has that intense goofy laugh. He's in the smart-geek-friend category of people, but not hot-date material. No, there's something else going on with Carole. Whatever it is, though, isn't good.

At least there's one bright spot in my life. I've gone to visit Mr. Aniso in the hospital a few times, and he's getting better. We've even gotten kind of friendly. Mostly I just sit and listen to his stories. He likes telling me about his life and I guess he's happy that I like to listen. He comes from a small town in Maine. His parents grew potatoes. He had to help out on the farm but he hated it. So he left to become a priest. That didn't work out either, so he decided to teach. "Heck, I knew all that Latin, so why not put it to good use and teach it to kids like you, who really appreciate it," he said once. We both had a good laugh over that one.

It's too bad he left the priesthood, though, because I think he would be a good priest. Sometimes we talk about religion. He has his doubts about God too. He calls God the Force, the Force of Love. He says it's good not to think of God as a person, but as something more amorphous and all-encompassing. Amorphous. I like that word and Mr. Aniso's theory about God. It reminds me of one of my favorite old movies, *Star Wars*, when they say "May the Force be with you." Mr. Aniso has never seen *Star Wars*, so I told him I'd get him a DVD which he could watch when he gets better.

One thing we don't talk about is anything to do with being gay. Apart from the time during my first visit when he told me he was gay, he doesn't bring it up. And I'm certainly not going to ask him about it, though in some ways I have to admit I'd like to. He's the first gay person I've known. And I guess I would like to find out what his life is like. I haven't seen any other visitors, and he hasn't mentioned anyone coming. Maybe that's just as well. What would I say to them?

*

Boy, I never knew spin the bottle could change your life! But it did mine, this weekend.

Let me start at the beginning. I went over to Carole's house Saturday afternoon. I thought we were just going to hang out as usual, maybe come up with some new ways of getting our computer business going again. And then I was hoping we could stop by at Joe's Pizza and act kissy-pervy like Bobby and Cynthia, and stuff pizza in our mouths. Anything to get our make-out sessions back on track.

But when I got to Carole's house she was there with Tim. She seemed in a good mood, smiling when she saw me, but maybe she was smiling because Tim was there. Who knows? We sat around for a while, and soon started talking about our computer business.

"Tim had a good idea about our advertising," Carole said. "We've got to think demographics."

"Demographics?" I turned to Tim.

"Yes, demographics," he said, in that nervous fast way he talks. "We haven't been thinking demographics."

He and Carole exchanged excited looks. I waited for him to continue, but then Carole burst in. "You see, Tim pointed out we haven't been advertising enough in the right places."

"We haven't?"

"No. Who uses our services mostly?"

"Well, people..."

"What kind of people?"

"What kind of people? I don't know. People who aren't good with computers..."

"And?"

I wasn't sure what Carole was driving at.

"What kind of people aren't good with computers? Old people, right?"

"Well, I know some old people who know about computers."

"Well, of course there are some!" Carole sounded impatient. "But a lot of them don't. And we need to target them."

"You mean like instead of Facebook and Twitter we go to nursing homes?"

"Well, not exactly." Tim finally spoke again. "But more places where older people hang out regularly. Like supermarkets. Or doctors' offices. Or stores where mothers go to buy diapers. Find places where we can put up signs. Big signs."

"And even online," Carole added. "Being on Facebook is okay, but I don't know how many people who need computer help are on Facebook. Like your mother. Is she on Facebook?"

I shook my head. "She tries, but not much lately I don't think. She's too busy working at Neiman Marcus and then spending time at her jewelry business."

"See," Carole said. "That's my point. But I bet she Googles. If we could only get our website to show up higher on Google searches."

We talked some more about Google and demographics. It all seemed a little pie-in-the-sky to me, but Carole and Tim seemed really excited by it, so I was willing to go along. Finally, even they got tired of talking about it. We sat around some more, and then Carole brought out an empty juice bottle.

"It's time for spin the bottle!"

I looked at Tim. He hadn't been too excited about spin the bottle before, but now he looked like he was ready to play.

"A new rule!" announced Carole. She was getting that little sparkly look in her eyes. "If the bottle points at you and you don't want to kiss, you can do that... But you have to take off a piece of clothing."

"What?"

"Yes. It's kind of like spin the bottle and strip poker combined."

"How far do we go?" Tim asked. I was glad he looked a little nervous now.

"As far as we want," Carole answered.

"As far as we want?"

"Sure. Where's your sense of adventure?"

"My sense of adventure?"

"Oh, come on. I said you can pass your turn on to the next person," Carole said, knowing Tim and I wouldn't be kissing each other. She sounded almost disappointed, though of course that meant she'd be doing all the kissing.

I couldn't come up with another good argument, and I guess neither could Tim. Carole spun the bottle and it pointed to me.

I leaned over and kissed Carole on the lips. Before I could move away, she grabbed me and kissed back, pressing her lips on mine in a long, slow kiss.

I stayed with her, kissing back until I couldn't breathe. We both let go, finally, gasping for air.

"Mmm, not bad," Carole said, giggling. "Seven point five out of ten."

"Are we rating the kisses too?"

"Sure, why not?"

I glanced over at Tim. He didn't seem nervous anymore, looking like he was ready to play.

"Come on, come on," Carole said to me. "Your turn."

I spun the bottle. It pointed to Tim.

"I pass," I said, the old blush coming on.

Tim looked relieved. Carole was giggling, obviously enjoying herself. "Okay, what are you taking off?"

I thought for a second and took off my right shoelace.

"Very good." Carole clapped her hands. "Tim, your turn."

Tim spun the bottle and it ended up pointing at Carole. Before I knew it, they were French kissing, big time. Their mouths were open, and their hands were all over each other's bodies, and I could tell their tongues were going at it too. This was Tim? With the huge zits and annoying voice, kissing Carole like that?

"Six point two," I said when they finally finished and looked to me for a score.

"Six point two! What was wrong with it?" Tim actually sounded upset.

"It didn't have enough artistic merit," I said, making something up. Was I jealous?

Carole quickly took the bottle and spun it. It pointed to Tim. So there they were, kissing again. This French kiss took even longer. Tim's hands went up and down Carole's back and front. Carole's hands were all over Tim too. That's when I knew this wasn't the first time they had French kissed.

"Five point zero," I said when they finished.

"What!"

Even Carole looked upset.

I shrugged. "I was watching your hands. They went out of bounds. You get penalties for that."

"Who said?"

"That wasn't in our rules."

"It is now."

We argued about that for a while. Even though I wasn't serious, I didn't want to give in. It was getting me mad that Carole and Tim were so into it. And they had been French kissing behind my back.

We continued the game, and when it was my turn with Carole, we tried to French kiss too. But it wasn't the same, even though I tried to feel her up for as long as Tim had.

"Three point five," Tim said. "Your kiss lacked passion."

Carole didn't say anything, and I turned away. I couldn't argue with Tim. Secretly I agreed with him. And I was glad when we had to end the game and the only things that had been taken off were my right shoelace and Tim's watch. Carole's mother had come home and needed her for something. Going home, I promised myself this would be my last game of spin the bottle with Carole, maybe with anybody.

*

Last night was a bust. At least for me. Carole's rules on spin the bottle worked out best for her, as I knew they would. She got kissed all the time, sometimes by me and mostly by Tim. Lucky Carole. Lucky Tim. I kept trying really hard, but I could have sworn Carole liked Tim's kisses more than mine.

So what was going on? It pissed me off, and I felt like a real loser. And now another Saturday night home alone when I'm already feeling like a loser. Forget the spring of my discontent. It's now the spring of my despair.

But I'm fighting it. When I woke up this morning, I decided to do the mature thing. I called Carole and asked if we could get together—alone. I told her I wanted to talk to her about something.

She sounded kind of hesitant at first, like she wasn't sure if she wanted to see me, but then she agreed.

"Come on over," she said.

"When?"

"How about later this afternoon? I have to finish some homework first."

Another sign of being a loser. A girl prefers to do her homework instead of seeing you.

"Okay," I said. "I'll be over later."

I did my own homework, hung out for a while to make sure I wasn't too early, and then I went over to Carole's house in the afternoon. She was smiling when she greeted me at the door, but it wasn't the little sparkly look she gets when she means business. It was more like the polite, phony smile people put on when they're trying to cover up something.

"Would you like some hot chocolate, RV?" Carole asked when I came inside. She even sounded phony.

I shook my head. "No." I'd decided to get right to the point. She wasn't going to get any phoniness from me. We sat on the couch. Neither of us said anything. It was crazy. Carole and I not knowing what to say to each other? That had never happened.

"Um, Carole," I finally said, sucking in my breath. "I'm sorry if I acted a little bit like a jerk last night."

"No, it's okay. Don't worry about it." Carole seemed like she didn't want to talk about it.

"No, no. It's not okay. I can't believe I took the game so seriously."

"We were just having fun."

"Well, some of us were."

"What do you mean?"

Despite my nerves, I was determined to say what I had gone there to say. "Well, you and Tim looked like you were having fun."

"Yeah. Weren't you?"

"Not really."

"Oh."

"I wasn't because... Well, because you and Tim were really into it. Like you were really into each other."

It was Carole's turn to look nervous. She glanced away and didn't say anything.

"I thought you and I were special. Going out together and all."

Carole was quiet, staring down at the floor for a long time. Then she looked up at me. "I thought we were...special too."

"So what happened?"

Carole shrugged. "I don't know exactly. I thought you didn't care anymore."

"Me, didn't care? What gave you that idea?"

"I don't know. Just a feeling I had."

"A feeling?"

"Yes. We haven't seen much of each other. And when we do get together, you're...well, you're distant."

"Distant?"

"Yes."

She coughed, looking uncomfortable, but then continued. "I know you said you have a lot on your mind. I thought that might have to do with me."

I didn't know what to say. Carole was picking up on all my confusion and questions about Bobby Marshall. I was angry at him for screwing up my life and for putting me in this position now with Carole.

"I'm sorry if I ever made you feel that way," I told her. "I didn't mean to. I really didn't." I shook my head. "But I wish you could've said something to me about what you were feeling before, before..." I didn't know how to finish the sentence and just stared at her.

Carole nodded, but she didn't say anything either.

"So are we okay?" I finally asked.

Carole was looking guilty. "Okay?"

"Yeah, you know..."

"You mean like friends? Sure, we're friends."

"That's not what I meant. I meant going out."

Okay. I was putting it out there. Asking her if we were going out.

Carole looked down at the floor again and kept quiet.

It took a few moments, but then I realized what she was trying to tell me. "So you and Tim are going out now?"

Carole nodded. "Well, we're not exactly going out, but—"

"But what?"

Carole didn't seem to know how to answer me. So much for her being the kind of person who wouldn't keep things from me.

Carole couldn't look at me. "I'm sorry, RV. I guess we are going out," she said, still avoiding my gaze. "I did want to say something to you. I've been trying to find the right time to talk to you about us. When I thought you weren't interested anymore, I started spending more time with Tim. And... And we realized we liked each other." She had a tremble in her voice, like she was about to cry.

"I see." But I didn't see at all.

We sat there like two mute puppets, not talking and not looking at each other. I couldn't believe things between me and Carole were over. Just like that. Before they ever really got started.

"I still hope we'll see each other," Carole said, not sounding very convinced that we would. "And there's our computer business."

"Yes. There's that."

We sat there for a little while longer making stupid small talk. I finally stood up to go.

"Okay. I guess I'll see you around."

Carole grabbed me by the shoulders. "RV, I really meant what I said. I—I want to stay friends."

"Yeah, me too," I said. I took Carole's hands off my shoulders and turned around to go. "Bye."

"Bye."

*

So what am I going to do with my life? Carole is gone. Bobby Marshall is somewhere far away in his thoughts. I feel like I'm gone too. Gone somewhere—to a place I don't exist. I've been trying to do some studying for the last hour, but I just can't get into it. Even going to the ball field to watch the jocks doesn't interest me anymore. It's more like a joke now. Clear to me that the world on the ball field has nothing to do with my world. And what's more, it never will.

*

"Mr. Aniso. What do you do when you feel like the only person in the world?"

I asked Mr. Aniso the question when I went to visit him today. I'm glad to say he's doing better. Some of his bandages are off and he said he can move around a little more in the bed.

Mr. Aniso sat up a little more. "What makes you say you're the only person in the world, RV?"

I told him about breaking up with Carole. "And, well, I thought I was becoming friends with Bobby Marshall, but I don't think he has much time for me since he's been going out with Cynthia Hoevermeyer." I hoped I wasn't blushing too much when I told him about Bobby, since it wasn't the whole story. Not by a long shot.

"They were your closest friends?" Mr. Aniso asked.

I nodded.

"You don't have other friends at school?"

I shrugged. "There are people I talk to and hang out with sometimes, but I'd call them acquaintances. Not real friends."

"What about at home?"

"Same story." I shrugged again. "I'm a real loser, aren't I?"

He reached out and grabbed my shoulder again. It happened so fast. I guess Mr. Aniso could move even better than he said he could. He was sitting up straight in the bed, gripping my shoulder hard, and he was staring at me in this intent, fixed way, I almost thought he was angry with me.

"RV, can you promise me one thing?"

He was gripping me so hard I couldn't do anything but nod.

"Never, ever, call yourself a loser. Okay? Never. Can you promise me that?"

I nodded again.

"Because you're not a loser. You're a great kid with a lot of great attributes and you have a great future ahead of you."

"Well, thanks, but—"

"Uh-uh, no buts. Promise me."

"I promise."

Mr. Aniso finally released his hand and sat back against his pillow. He was breathing heavily, trying to catch his breath. I guess he still couldn't move as well as he thought he could.

Mr. Aniso lay quietly for a while, staring up at the ceiling, and I wondered what was going on in his thoughts. Then he turned to me.

"It's hard when you feel alone," he said, "even though usually you're not as alone as you think you are." He paused. I didn't say anything, so he continued. "But I know. Sometimes you have many feelings going on inside, but because there's no one to share them with you get lost in them. Is that how you feel?"

"Sort of."

After a while, he sat up a little again, making himself more comfortable. "RV. Let me tell you a little story. About myself." He was staring at me again in that intense way, and all I could do was stare back.

"Remember how I told you I was studying to be a priest, but it didn't work out?"

"Uh-huh."

"Well, the reason was because I fell in love with another student. And he was in love with me. Or so I thought." He paused, I'm sure to see how I'd react. I didn't say anything, though I wouldn't be surprised if I was blushing, at least a little bit.

"Well, word got around the seminary," Mr. Aniso said, continuing his story. "And we were summoned to the rector's office."

"That's like the principal's office?"

"Yeah. Kind of. Except the rector has the Pope backing him up. And the Pope has God." Mr. Aniso couldn't help smiling. "Our headmaster at Latin school doesn't claim to have that much authority, at least not so far."

We both laughed. "Not so far."

"What happened?"

"We were questioned and given a choice. Give up each other or give up God. That's how the rector put it to us. Give up each other or give up God."

"So you both left the seminary?"

Mr. Aniso shook his head. "No. I left. My friend stayed."

"So he gave you up."

"I guess he did." Mr. Aniso looked sad and thought for a second. "And in the beginning I thought I had given up God because I left the seminary." He gave me a sharp look. "And you can imagine how alone you feel when you think you've given up God."

I nodded, thinking about my own questions about the Big Guy.

"It took me time, a long time, to learn I didn't have to give up God to find myself," Mr. Aniso continued. "But boy, until I learned that, it was hard."

"So are you saying I'm going through something like that?"

"Yes, I think so," Mr. Aniso said, looking like he really meant it. "You're not as alone as you think you are, RV. One never is. Though I know sometimes it surely feels like it."

I thought for a second. "Mr. Aniso, can I ask you something?"

He nodded.

"Are you glad you left the seminary?"

He smiled. "You don't know how many times I've asked myself that question."

"And what did you answer?"

He smiled again. "The word glad doesn't come into it. I had no choice, even if the rector said I did. I had to do it in order not to give up on myself. But the best thing I learned is that God never gave up on me, even if I thought I had given up on Him."

I must have looked puzzled because Mr. Aniso smiled at me.

"I know what I'm saying might not make sense to you now, RV. But believe me, someday it will." He reached out and touched me on the shoulder again, but this time it was a gentle pat. "Don't feel bad about all the questions going through your mind. Let them come. Someday the answers will come too."

I looked up at him. He was smiling at me. And he looked very happy. And I suddenly didn't feel alone. Not by a long shot.

Chapter Seventeen

Secrets

When I walked into the kitchen this evening for dinner, Mom and Dad were already at the table talking. They weren't squabbling for a change, but talking quietly. I wish quiet would mean something good in our house, but I never know what to expect. Sure enough, Mom and Dad stopped talking as soon as I walked into the room.

"*Labas vakaras*. Good evening," I said, trying to sound as nonchalant as possible. (That word does come in handy!)

Dad said Mom got a loan for her jewelry business. I couldn't tell if he was upset or happy about it.

"Congratulations!" I said in English, looking at Mom.

Mom had a triumphant smile on her face. "Thank you," she said in English, with a little bow of her head. She seemed very pleased. She told us that after thinking about it, she didn't want to use up money from the house savings account. She first wanted to try to get the money another way. So she went to the bank after seeing an ad about small business loans and asked for a loan for $2500. She had filled out a lot of forms and had to go back for some interviews a couple of times. Everyone she talked to had been encouraging, but she hadn't heard anything, so she had given up hope. Until today. The loan came through today. Mom held up a piece of paper.

"Wow, that's great, Mom," I said again. I hadn't seen her so happy in a long time.

Dad asked her about the terms of the loan.

Mom told him the terms were good. And she could now put the $2500 back in the savings account, so Dad wouldn't have to worry. She seemed very pleased with herself.

Dad looked like he wanted to say something but didn't know what, so he didn't say anything. I held my breath, keeping my fingers crossed that he wouldn't say anything to spoil our celebratory mood.

But then Ray walked into the room, and everyone's attention turned to him. He had a big black-and-blue mark under his left eye.

Mom jumped up. *"Kas atsitiko?"* "What happened?"

Ray shrugged. *"Nieko."* "Nothing."

"Nu, kaip nieko?" "What do you mean nothing?" Dad looked both concerned and angry.

Ray told us he hurt himself. Dad wanted to know how. Ray said he accidentally walked into a telephone pole.

That didn't sit too well with Dad. He told Ray the last time he'd checked, Ray's eyes were in the front of his head, not the back.

That didn't sit too well with Mom. She told Dad to stop the sarcasm.

Dad told her to stop finding excuses for Ray.

I guess we couldn't avoid a dinner without at least a little nit-picking. Ray did let Mom apply an ice pack to his face. But he stuck with his story when she asked him a second time what happened. Dad just grumbled and turned silent.

After dinner I went to Ray's room. He was lying on his bed not doing anything. That was odd because he usually has his headphones on, listening to music. Sometimes he's flipping through a comic book. Tonight he was doing neither.

"What do you want?" he asked.

"I just came to see if you're okay."

"I'm fine, thanks."

"You sure? That looks like a nasty bruise."

"It looks worse than it is."

"You sure?"

"Yes, I'm sure."

So much for my attempt at brotherly bonding. I was about to turn around and leave his room when I noticed a wad of bills sticking out of Ray's pants pocket.

"What's that?"

"What's what?"

"That." I nodded toward his pocket.

Ray moved his body, trying to hide the money better. But instead the entire wad fell out of the pocket onto the bed.

I just stared at it. Ray quickly took it and stuffed it back into his pocket.

"Wow. Where did you get all that money?" I asked. I was genuinely impressed, even though I didn't really want to know the answer because I knew it couldn't be good.

Ray shrugged. "It's not mine."

"What do you mean it's not yours?"

"I'm holding it for a friend."

"A friend? Why?"

"Will you stop asking me all these questions. You're not Dad."

"And aren't you glad I'm not. If he saw you with that—" I stopped myself. For a visit that started out as an attempt at brotherly bonding, this was turning into another fight. Didn't we have enough of them in this house? "Okay. Sorry, Ray. I was just a little worried, that's all." I turned to go a second time.

"RV, it's not what you think it is." Ray sounded like he had softened, just a little bit.

"I don't know what I'm thinking, Ray." I turned back to look at him. "Sorry for the older brother routine."

"RV. I'm not in trouble, if that's what you're thinking. No one's in trouble. No one's doing anything underhanded. No one's doing anything illegal!"

"Okay. I'm glad." I fumbled for the right words. "I'm really glad. Because... Well, I'm losing all my friends these days, and I'd feel horrible if I lost you too."

"Thanks."

"I mean it."

"I mean it too."

*

I have this dream. I've been dreaming it a lot lately. I'm sitting in the first car of a roller coaster, and we're about to start going. But it turns out I'm driving, and when I look back at the rest of the roller coaster the other cars are empty. But just before we start moving Mom rushes up and gets into the car behind me. I start to push the pedal to take off but then Dad rushes up and sits behind Mom. I want to start again but then Ray rushes up. And then other people I know rush up too. Like Carole. And Bobby. I start to lose patience waiting for everyone, but then we go. Everyone is hanging on really tightly because they don't trust my driving. I'm not worried, though, and I love the view when we go up and down the hills. But then we get up to the biggest hill and start going down, and I realize I don't know how to stop the roller coaster. We keep going down, faster and faster. I keep trying to find the brake, but I can't. We're still going down. Different people start flying out of the cars. Then I wake up.

I had the dream again tonight. Tonight everyone flew out of the cars and I was the only one left. What does it mean? Am I losing my entire family! My life? Things better change fast or I'm afraid it will happen in reality.

*

Oh, man. What can I say? I still have to process everything that happened today.

Bobby called me up last night and said he needed a special favor. Something about reading a book report he did for English. I said sure, I could do it next week.

"I was hoping you'd be able to do it this weekend."

"Is the book report late?"

"No. But it's due Monday."

I was happy he called, even though things have changed between us. But there was something about the way he said it was due Monday that made me think he wasn't telling the truth. I didn't want to say anything though. I'm already becoming too jaded about all the secrets in my family. I don't need to worry about Bobby Marshall's secrets too. (Jaded, my new favorite word, although I wish it wasn't. It sort of means nothing surprises you about what people do anymore because they do a lot of rotten things. Sad but true. But that's reality. Here's another title for my autobiography. I can call it *The Jaded World of RV.*)

Anyway, since it's Saturday, I agreed to meet him in the afternoon at Joe's Pizza after his baseball practice. (Is there a sport this guy can't play?) I wondered if he'd bring Cynthia along. But I decided not to say anything about that either. I'd play it cool. The new, jaded RV at your service.

But when Bobby showed up at Joe's, he was alone. I'd come a little early, and was already eating a slice and reading a book.

"Hi," Bobby said.

"Oh, hi."

He looked a little uncomfortable, like the last time, not sure if he should sit or not. I moved my stuff, making room for him in the booth. Once he did sit down, though, it felt just like the good old days. I have to admit my heart did a little pitter-patter when he sat down across from me. But then the jaded RV took over again, and I reminded myself to get over it and face reality.

"How was practice?"

Bobby shrugged. "Oh, fine. It will take some time for the team to learn to play together but we'll get there."

I nodded. I didn't have the faintest idea of what it took for a baseball team to get it together, so didn't say anything.

"So, how have you been, RV?"

"Oh, fine. Doing a lot of work for school. Some of the teachers are really piling on the work."

"Yeah. Maybe they feel we're behind so they want to fit everything in before the school year ends."

"Yeah, maybe."

We chitchatted about that for a while. "So, do you have your book report?" I finally asked.

"Oh, yeah." Bobby took out a paper from the gear bag he had brought. It was rolled up and crinkled at the edges. "Thanks for reading it. It's on *The Great Gatsby*. We had to write about what we thought of the book. I just hope I made sense... And don't forget the typos," he added as he got up to get some pizza.

Maybe I couldn't concentrate, but Bobby's report seemed fine to me. I told him so after I'd read it and he had returned and finished eating.

"You sure?"

"Yeah. I feel that way about the book too. Who cares about some rich guys partying."

"But isn't it about the American Dream?"

"I guess so. What is the American Dream?"

"Yeah. What is it?"

We talked about that for a while. Bobby got a faraway look in his eyes, which surprised me. If there was anyone who would have the American Dream down cold, it would be Bobby Marshall.

We started walking toward home. Bobby was quiet, but I could tell something was on his mind. I wondered if there was a problem with Cynthia. I wanted to ask, and yet didn't want to know at the same time. But finally, I couldn't stand it any longer.

"How's Cynthia?" I tried to sound nonchalant, but you know how that is. The more you try the less nonchalant you sound.

"Cynthia and I broke up the other day," Bobby answered.

"Oh, I'm sorry to hear that." Why do people lie? Why was I lying?

We walked on in silence for a while. Then Bobby turned to me. "I'm the one who broke it off, actually."

"Oh?"

"Yeah. It just wasn't working."

"I know how that is."

"You do?"

"Well, from the other side. I guess Carole felt the same way. That's why she broke up with me."

"Oh, I'm sorry to hear it."

"Yeah, I was too. But things have been a little weird between Carole and me for a while, so I shouldn't have been surprised."

"Weird? In what way?"

"Just weird." How could I explain it to Bobby? I still couldn't really explain it well to myself.

Bobby thought for a while. "Yeah, I guess I felt the same way. Things were weird between me and Cynthia."

Without even discussing it, Bobby and I had made our way to the woods—to the same spot by the stream where I'd spent time with Carole and then him. I grew nervous remembering how sad I'd felt the last time we were there. I didn't want to feel sad again.

I suggested we go somewhere else. Bobby seemed a little surprised, but didn't argue.

We walked deeper into the woods and found some big boulders in a clearing. You could still see the hills in the distance above the trees. I suddenly realized why I liked seeing those hills. They make me feel good about what's out in the world and the future, like it belongs to me, too, not just everybody else.

The sun beating down on our faces felt good. I pointed out the fresh green leaves on the trees to Bobby.

"Yeah. Makes you feel optimistic about life, doesn't it?" He didn't look very optimistic though.

"What are you thinking about?" I asked.

"I was just thinking about the last time we met. And you told me about how you felt different and you didn't really fit into any one place. Remember that?"

"Yeah."

"Do you still feel the same way?"

"A lot."

"Yeah. I'm sorry I didn't really get what you were saying." He gave me a quick look. "Or maybe I did and didn't want to hear it."

"What do you mean?"

"Well, because I sometimes feel that way too. But I guess I didn't want to admit it."

"You? The football-basketball-hockey-baseball-and-everything-else jock?" I was sorry as soon as the words flew out of my mouth, but it was too late to take them back.

"Oh, not you too! Just because I like sports doesn't mean I'm a dumb jock!" He looked angry.

"I'm sorry. I didn't mean that."

"I hope you didn't. You know how I feel about that with my father and all." He softened a bit. "I have other parts to my life, you know. Parts that make me feel different. Like everyone does."

"You're right. Like me too. Why do we stereotype people so easily?"

"I don't know."

We sat there not saying anything for a while, both of us lost in our own thoughts. I looked over at the hills in the distance and thought about my roller coaster dream. The good part. On a sunny day like today, with the sky so blue, the view from the coaster would be spectacular. Bobby asked me what I was thinking about, and I told him about that part of my dream.

He laughed—for the first time today it seemed.

"Was I in the roller coaster too?" he asked.

I nodded, laughing too.

"Good. Because I would trust your driving."

"Don't be so sure." Then I thought about the other part of the dream and told Bobby about it.

"What do you think it means?"

"Beats me. Maybe I'm afraid of all those other parts of my life that bring me down."

"What parts?" Bobby had turned to me, looking very serious.

I could feel myself blush. "Parts that make me feel different."

Bobby was nodding. "Yes." Then he looked up at me again. "What makes you feel different?"

I remembered the last time Bobby and I had a similar conversation. Was I going to beat around the bush again?

"Well, I feel different about the people I like."

"You mean friends?"

"I mean romantically."

Bobby looked embarrassed. But instead of stopping me, it made me want to keep talking.

"You know how some people are gay and all?"

"Yes." Bobby couldn't meet my gaze, clasping and unclasping his hands.

"I sometimes feel that."

"You mean the gay stuff?"

"Yeah."

Bobby looked up at me. "Me too."

"You too?"

"Yeah."

We were both quiet, but my heart was beating so loudly I was sure it would fly out of my chest at any minute. Did I just hear what I think I heard? Bobby told me he might be gay too?

"Not that I don't like girls or anything," Bobby said suddenly. "I enjoyed making out with Cynthia and stuff. That's not why we broke up."

"I know what you mean. I enjoyed making out with Carole."

"So what makes you think you might be gay?" Bobby asked me.

"I—I'm not sure exactly. But I notice guys and think about them a lot...and other stuff." I couldn't bring myself to tell him how much I thought about him.

Bobby was quiet for a while. "So what makes a person gay?"

I shrugged. "Do you think I know? And if you like girls, too, doesn't that make you bi?"

Bobby shook his head. "All these labels. All these questions. Why can't people just be themselves?"

I shrugged again. "Yeah, but what is being yourself? I'm still trying to figure that out."

"Yeah, I guess you're right. I am too," Bobby said.

We both started laughing. We sat and laughed for a long time. I guess all the stuff we've been keeping in for so long was now coming out in waves and waves of laughter. We talked more about how we'd been keeping everything in and denying it. I told Bobby about my visits to the hospital with Mr. Aniso and how he made me feel better about gay people. Bobby told me that's why he'd gone out with Cynthia because he didn't want to think about any gay feelings. We talked about a lot of other things too. And we both have a lot of questions. But it was so amazing to just laugh and joke and let go of our secrets. Some of them anyway. You don't know how bad holding secrets feels until you let go of them.

*

So Bobby might be gay. Like I said, I'm still having trouble processing that. Life suddenly feels positive. Funny how it can change so fast. Jaded RV is gone. Maybe my autobiography now should be *The Optimistic World of RV.*

Whoa! Whoa! I've got to stop that! Haven't I been in this position before? Really excited—and then I get brought back down to earth. Dashed down is more like it. I have to remember the Big Guy. What does it say in the Bible? He gives with one hand. And He takes away with the other one. I sure know how that works! He's played enough tricks on me. Haven't you, Big Guy? But please, please, let me enjoy this for a little while at least. And don't make me do anything stupid to spoil it. Maybe that's what going down in the roller coaster dream is all about. If something bad happens between me and Bobby now, I think it will be just like the dream. I'll keep going down and will never get up.

Chapter Eighteen

Complications

Am I always going to feel like two people? Or maybe three. Or more.

After talking to Bobby I feel like sharing our secrets with the whole world. Shouting to whoever will listen. "Hey, world! I like Bobby! And Bobby likes me! And I'm getting to know Mr. Aniso better. He's gay—and a great guy!"

It's like I'm a different person. I don't want to make excuses anymore. I want to tell everyone about what's really happening in my life.

But that's inside. The outside part of me hasn't changed at all. I still have to do my homework. I still have my frozen moments at dinner. I'm still scared of Duffy and Doyle. And in a lot of other ways I'm still the same crazy person I've always been.

As a matter of fact sometimes I have a hard time believing any of it is happening. Bobby and I had that talk a few days ago, but he hasn't been in class and I haven't seen him since. Now I'm starting to think I dreamed the whole thing. Or maybe I didn't dream it, but Bobby changed his mind or realizes he made a mistake and he likes Cynthia after all. I don't know. I'm just sure of one thing. Everything—and everyone—around me is just the same, and different, and screwed up as always.

Today at dinner Dad was in a sour mood. What else is new? This time he lectured us about Russia and China, how they were going to take over the world. Ever since I can remember they've been getting ready to take over the world. They must be slow in getting around to it, though, because it hasn't happened yet.

Even Mom was in a sour mood. She's started working a couple of nights in downtown Boston, trying to sell her jewelry, but she doesn't seem happy. She says it's more work than she thought, and she doesn't like the owner she's renting the space from.

And Ray, forget Ray. If he ever smiles or says he's happy at dinner, I'll know he's taking drugs.

"And how are you doing, RV?"

"Me? Oh, pretty good, Mom. I'm becoming good friends with Bobby."

"Bobby?"

"Yeah. Bobby. The guy who came to dinner. The jock. He and I had a nice talk the other day about how we both might be gay."

"That's nice."

"Yeah. Very nice. It's good to have a friend who might be gay too. Just like me."

Wouldn't that be a great conversation? Great fantasy, RV. Too bad it ain't gonna happen.

Yeah, too bad. No. If I said anything like that at dinner Mom and Dad's reaction would be pretty different. Especially Dad's. There was something about gay marriage on TV the other day, and I saw the dark look come into Dad's eyes. Plus a few words in Russian I didn't understand. But I bet they weren't complimentary.

I sometimes think I could talk to Mom about it. But I'd have to get over her crying first. She'd cry because the church still doesn't approve of gays. Especially the Lithuanian church. Last week at Mass, the priest was going on about the breakdown of morals. He talked about murderers, prostitutes, and gays, and how they were ruining the world. I wanted to tell him Christ hung out with prostitutes, but I didn't dare.

Nope. I'll just have to continue to smile and keep quiet during our family dinners. At least it's better than another frozen moment.

I just thought of something. Is keeping quiet like one long frozen moment? That's depressing. I'm not going to think about that right now. I can't. I'm feeling too good to let myself get depressed. I want to think about Bobby and when I'm going to see him next. I wonder if he's thinking the same thing about me.

*

I finally saw Bobby today in school. It wasn't what I expected—or hoped for.

Bobby was in the hall, talking to Cynthia. It was between classes, and there were a lot of kids around, so it was easy for me to be inconspicuous. (Inconspicuous. It means you're almost invisible. Another one of my specialties.)

Anyway, Bobby and Cynthia seemed to be having a serious conversation. Actually, it was more like Cynthia was doing the talking and Bobby was listening. And nodding. She would say something, and he would nod his head. Then she'd say something else, and he'd nod again. Neither of them looked very happy.

Biology class was right afterward. I said "hi" to Bobby as nonchalantly as I could.

"Hi," Bobby said, but he still looked upset.

"How's it going? You missed a couple of classes."

"Yeah, I know. I had a cold."

Bobby Marshall, missing class because of a cold? I didn't quite buy it, but Bobby didn't look like he wanted to explain anything.

And that was the extent of our conversation. We sat there in class, staring straight ahead, as Mr. Swenson, the Biology teacher, told us about our final project for the year. We were going to cut up frogs and spend time studying what we found.

A couple of kids made faces. Mr. Swenson explained that the frogs were being kept in formaldehyde, which was a strong smell and might take some getting used to.

One kid raised his hand and said he was allergic to formaldehyde. Mr. Swenson told him they would talk after class. Another kid said he was a vegetarian. Mr. Swenson said he didn't expect us to cook and eat the frogs. Everyone laughed.

Except Bobby. He was still in his own world at the end of the class, not looking at me.

"So, Bobby. I guess I'll see you around," I said when we were gathering up our books.

"Yeah. I guess."

"Do you...do you need any help with papers or anything?"

"No. Not now. I'm fine now," Bobby said. Then he turned around and walked away.

I kind of stood there for a few seconds, feeling like a jerk.

"Hey, RV. What's the matter?"

It was Whalen, the guy who thinks of me as an angel.

I shook my head. "Nothing. Why?"

"You look like you're ready to cry. Like you've been dumped by a girl."

"I'm not even going out with anyone," I said, trying to look more cheerful.

"Too bad," Whalen said. "So why are you looking like that?"

*

I went to see Mr. Aniso today. When I walked into his room, he was walking back and forth, supported by a nurse. He was moving slowly, but he was definitely moving.

"Hey, RV. Look at me!" he said. His voice sounded stronger too.

"Hey, Mr. Aniso. That's great."

Mr. Aniso gestured to the nurse. "RV, meet Maria, the best nurse in the world!"

Maria giggled. She was really small, with the darkest hair and darkest eyes I've ever seen. I had no idea how she could prevent Mr. Aniso from falling if he lost his balance, but I guess that's what they learn in nursing school.

Maria led Mr. Aniso to a chair and helped him sit down. She motioned for me to sit in another chair next to his.

"There. You've had your exercise so now you can relax and talk to your visitor," Maria said to Mr. Aniso. "I will leave you two alone." Then she turned to me. "Can I get you anything?" she asked. "Some water? We also have soda."

I started to shake my head, but Mr. Aniso interrupted me. "Oh, RV, go for it. I want to celebrate today."

"Okay, I'll have a Coke, please," I said to Maria and she left the room, telling me she'd be right back with it.

I turned to Mr. Aniso. "Did something good happen?"

"Yes, something good happened today. And all week. Look at me, sitting in this chair. And what was I doing when you walked into the room?"

"Walking? With Maria."

"Yes, walking." Mr. Aniso looked so excited I thought he was going to jump out of his chair and start dancing. "RV. You don't know what this means to me. Until about a week or so ago I wasn't sure I'd be able to walk on my own again."

He leaned closer to me and told me the injury to his legs was worse than he at first knew. Some muscles had been cut with a knife, very deeply. The doctors only told him that later.

He smiled again. "The physical therapy has been a bitch, but I couldn't be happier. I can walk!"

But I was still thinking about the knife. "So you weren't just roughed up a little? It was worse than that?"

"Yes, I guess it was." His smile seemed a little sad, but he was still smiling.

Maria came back with my Coke, and gave Mr. Aniso a cup with some liquid too.

"So, RV. How's everything at school?" Mr. Aniso asked after she left.

I shrugged. "It's okay."

"And how's Miss Carlson, I mean, the Milkmaid, doing?"

"Did I tell you that's what we call her?" I asked, feeling embarrassed.

"No, but I have some other sources," Mr. Aniso said mysteriously. He let out a little giggle that reminded me of Carole. It was nice to see him in such a good mood.

Thinking about Carole must have showed on my face because he suddenly turned serious. He asked me how things were going in that department. I shrugged. "The same," I said. "Pretty much nowhere."

"It takes a while, but things get better," Mr. Aniso said, encouragingly. "Remember what I told you last time? About what happened to me at the seminary?"

I nodded.

"There's always hope. That's what I learned from that experience. That's why I refuse to let this—" he motioned to himself. "That's why I refuse to let this get me down."

I nodded again. What he said reminded me of my conversation with Bobby. "One good thing happened to me," I said, after thinking for a minute.

"Oh?"

I knew I was at one of those moments of life where what you say could change everything.

"Well, I have this friend..." I finally said, looking down at the floor, not knowing whether I should mention Bobby by name. Then I remembered I had already told him about Bobby and Cynthia. "Well, Bobby Marshall. You know Bobby."

"Yes."

"Well, he broke up with Cynthia."

"I'm sorry for Bobby, but is that better for your friendship?" Mr. Aniso wanted to know.

"I don't know." I looked at the floor again. Why were these things so hard?

I looked back up. Mr. Aniso was regarding me patiently, waiting for an explanation.

"Well, we had a talk. And I told him... I told him that I was thinking about... That I might be...gay."

There. I'd said the word out loud for the second time in my life.

Mr. Aniso didn't react one way or the other. He just asked, "How did the conversation go?"

"Okay." I wanted to tell him Bobby was struggling with the same feelings, too, but Bobby had made me promise not to say anything, to anyone. On pain of death. These secrets are really strong, aren't they?

"What are you thinking about, RV?" Mr. Aniso was studying me intently.

I shrugged. "Oh, nothing. I was just thinking about my conversation with Bobby."

"And how did it feel to open up to him?" Mr. Aniso wanted to know.

"It felt scary, but good," I said.

"Yes, it does feel good, doesn't it?" Mr. Aniso smiled. "Though right before opening up to someone about yourself is so scary, isn't it?"

"Yes, but—" I said, interrupting him. "Things have been strange since." I told Mr. Aniso about seeing Bobby with Cynthia in the hallway, and how Bobby acted strange in class the other day.

"Maybe he's conflicted about his feelings toward Cynthia," Mr. Aniso suggested. "Romantic feelings take time to sort out because they're such a deep part of us." He thought for a second and then added, "And people have complicated feelings about gay friends. Give Bobby time."

"Yes," I said, nodding.

"You don't look like you believe me," Mr. Aniso said.

"I do believe you," I answered.

"But?"

"But, well, there's been so much going on, I don't know what to believe sometimes."

"What's been going on?"

So I told Mr. Aniso about going out with Carole and then breaking up with her. And praying to God. And seeing Duffy and Doyle pick on McGrath. And trying not to let Mom and Dad's arguing get me down. And trying not to think about Bobby but thinking about him even more. And trying to be a regular guy, and a good guy, but not always being able to live up to my expectations.

The secrets kept tumbling out. I couldn't tell Mr. Aniso more about Bobby, but I told him about so many other things, things that at one time I thought I could never tell anyone.

Mr. Aniso's hand clutched my shoulder. I realized I had been crying. The tears kept rolling down my cheeks and I kept trying to wipe them with the shirt sleeve of my other arm, embarrassed that Mr. Aniso was seeing me in this condition.

But he was gripping my shoulder as hard as he's ever gripped it and he wasn't letting go. "RV," he said, forcing me to meet his gaze. "Remember when I made you promise not to ever, ever call yourself a loser?"

I nodded.

"I hope you still remember that."

I nodded again.

"You're going to do great in life."

"What makes you say that?"

"Because just by telling me everything you've just told me, you're already starting to figure things out. You may not know it yet, but you are."

"If you say so."

"I know so. That's what life is all about. Trying to figure things out. Asking questions." Mr. Aniso took his cup and made me pick up my Coke can so he could toast it. Then he looked at me, starting to smile.

"Can you do me a big favor?"

"What?"

"Can you help me walk across the room a few more times?"

"Are you sure you have the energy?"

"Of course I have the energy! I want to celebrate our friendship."

"Our friendship?"

"Aren't we friends? You came to make me feel better when I was really bad during my early days in the hospital. And today you have made me feel great!"

"I have?"

"Yes."

"How?"

"Just by telling me more about yourself."

He smiled again. "That's what friends are for, aren't they? For sharing about themselves."

"I guess so."

"Yes," he said, laughing. "And someday you'll really believe me."

I helped Mr. Aniso get out of his chair. He felt surprisingly light. Maria wouldn't have had any problem lifting him up. I guess a few months in the hospital will do that to you.

I didn't know what to think walking slowly across the room, with Mr. Aniso leaning on me. Who was helping who more? I always thought of teachers helping us. And I know how much Mr. Aniso has helped me. But I didn't know it could go the other way.

*

"Hi, RV. It's me."

I didn't have to guess who "me" was. Bobby. He called me this morning. Even though I was a little upset with him, I was still glad to hear from him.

"Hey, Bobby. Good to hear from you."

Bobby was quiet for a few seconds, like he was trying to figure out what to say. "Sorry I've been...not around," he finally said. "I've had a lot on my mind."

"I know how that is."

"Listen. I need a favor."

"Are you having trouble writing another paper?" I couldn't help asking the question. I was wondering if the only reason Bobby wanted to be friends was for my help with his book reports and essays.

"How... How did you guess?" Bobby sounded a little uncomfortable. I can't say I felt bad about that. The old jaded RV coming back. "I'm...I'm sorry if you think I only call you when I need help with a paper," he said, like he was reading my thoughts. He sounded apologetic. Now I felt a little bad.

"No, it's okay. I know we're friends for a lot of reasons."

"Yes, we are." Bobby sounded more definite, which made me feel better. Then he was quiet again. "But I do need help with a history paper," he finally said.

"Oh, really?" I teased. I just can't be mad at Bobby. Not for long anyway. Even if he only likes me because of my writing, I'd always be happy to help him.

We made plans for me to go over his house. That's where I was tonight. Do I mind? Like I said, I can't be mad at him for long. He calls and I'm happy to help him any time.

But helping him with his paper was the least of it tonight.

I said hi to his parents, and then we went up to his room. There were a couple of books open on Bobby's bed, and some crumpled-up pieces of paper too. Bobby looked frustrated.

"I have to write a paper for history. We're up to the Renaissance, and we're supposed to write about something from that period. Something that still inspires people." He shook his head. "What do I know about the Renaissance? I can't even spell it."

I laughed. "Yeah, a lot of people have trouble spelling that. Even I did before." I told him we also had to do a paper on the Renaissance a few weeks ago.

"What did you write about?"

"*The Agony and the Ecstasy.*"

Bobby looked at me strangely.

I told him it was a book I read about how Michelangelo painted the Sistine Chapel in Rome. "The Pope made him do it. Michelangelo wanted to quit but the Pope wouldn't let him. So it shows you even geniuses have a hard time sometimes."

"I'm no genius." Bobby looked miffed. "Not like you."

"That's not what I meant," I answered. I hoped Bobby didn't think I was a snob. Can I help it if I like to read a lot of books? Even crazy ones? "Hey, I'm a dunce when it comes to throwing a football," I felt compelled to add. "So don't ever think you're worse than other people." And I put my hand on Bobby's shoulder, the way Mr. Aniso does with me.

Bobby brightened up a little, which made me feel glad. I suggested a few other things from the Renaissance that he could write about. We looked through his books, searching for a good topic, but Bobby rejected everything. He looked frustrated again.

"I guess I'll just have to take an extension on the paper," he finally said, throwing up his hands. "I just can't focus on this."

I urged him not to give up, reminding him of Michelangelo.

"I told you I'm no genius!" he yelled. He shut the book he was leafing through with a bang and threw it on the floor. I must have looked really shocked because he apologized right away. "Listen, I'm sorry, RV. I told you I've had a lot on my mind and I just can't concentrate on anything."

"It's okay."

"No. It's not okay. It really sucks."

I sat there, afraid to say anything. Was he going to tell me he had made up with Cynthia again? I was getting tired of that. Or was he changing his mind about what he told me in the woods? That his gay thoughts amounted to nothing?

Bobby was sitting at the edge of his bed just staring out into space. I was sitting in a chair next to the bed, feeling more and more uncomfortable. Finally, I couldn't take it any longer. "Are you and Cynthia back together again?" I asked.

He shook his head. "No. Though she wants us to." Then he added more quietly. "But I know it wouldn't be the right thing to do." He looked up at me. "I've just been thinking about our talk... You know... About the gay stuff." He shook his head. "I still can't believe it. Even that we talked about it."

"You mean our talk wasn't real. Like it didn't happen?"

"Yeah."

I nodded. "I've been thinking the same thing too," I couldn't help adding.

"I mean, how could I be gay? Why me?"

"I know. I ask myself that, too, sometimes," I told him.

"And other times?"

"And other times it feels okay. Like it's not such a big deal." I told him about my last visit with Mr. Aniso. "He makes me feel better about being gay."

"But he's such a femme type guy. And we're not like that."

"But that's just it," I said, shaking my head. "Mr. Aniso may be a femme, but when I'm with him it doesn't matter. The outside doesn't count as much. It's what's inside that counts more. The more I get to talk to him, the more I like him."

I couldn't help smiling after my little speech. I felt so adult and profound. I'm not sure if Bobby thought so, though, because he gave me a friendly shove. "You better be careful or you'll become as swishy as Mr. Aniso."

I shoved him back. "No I won't. You can bet on that."

Bobby turned serious again. "RV. If you are gay, are you worried about your parents finding out?"

"What do you think?" I said.

"I freak out just thinking about my father's face if I even mention the subject. Or my coaches. Or other people on my teams."

Bobby looked so depressed I went over to the bed and sat next to him. Instead of just grabbing him by the shoulder with one hand, I put my entire arm around his shoulder and hugged him. "It will be okay, Bobby. We've got to believe that." I couldn't help laughing at myself a little. Me, giving advice about being gay. What a joke. And yet somewhere down deep I believed it. I had to.

Bobby hugged me back. "I'm glad we talked that day in the woods, RV," he said. "Good to talk to someone about it. I've been going crazy. If I didn't have you to talk to, I don't know…" Then he put his hand down on the bed and it went on top of mine. Whether Bobby was too wrapped up in his thoughts to notice, or he did it intentionally, I couldn't tell. But his hand stayed on top of mine.

Why did any touch from Bobby feel so electric? That's the only word I can think of to describe it. Any time he touches a part of me it feels like he is touching my whole body.

Bobby finally removed his hand from mine. "What are you thinking about?" he asked, glancing at me and then looking away again.

I turned away too. "I'm just thinking about how much I'm blushing. And it makes me embarrassed."

"Don't be embarrassed. I'm blushing too."

I looked up at him. I couldn't see any signs of blushing on his cheeks.

"You're blushing? Black people blush, too, huh?"

Bobby gave me a sharp look.

"RV!"

"Sorry, I—"

"Another stupid stereotype. So you don't think black people blush?"

"I—I'm sorry. I don't know."

"Feel my face," Bobby said. "Feel it!" He took my hand, lifted it up to his cheek, and held it there. "What do you feel?"

"It feels warm. Hot."

"Because I'm blushing. Okay?"

"Okay."

"So, another stereotype blown to bits?"

"Yes."

He was still keeping my hand against his cheek. Holding it there for I don't know how long.

And he was staring at me, staring directly into my eyes, so that I was afraid to move or even breathe.

Finally he let my hand drop from his cheek and looked away. We sat there side by side, not saying anything for a long time. Then he slowly got up off the bed and went to retrieve the book he had thrown on the floor.

"I guess we better get back to the Renaissance," he said.

"Yes," I agreed, though I knew focusing on the Renaissance wasn't going to be easy for me either. I was still thinking about how it felt to touch his cheek and have him staring at me. I couldn't get any of it out of my mind.

Chapter Nineteen

Double Existence

Dinners at home have become really weird. It's like there are two RVs sitting at table. There's the usual, nice, polite RV who tries to eat all his vegetables and just stays quiet when everyone is arguing. Those frozen moments do come in handy.

Then there is the other RV. The crazy RV. The one who thinks about Bobby Marshall 24/7. The one who dreams about Bobby Marshall. The one who's afraid Bobby Marshall will take over his life.

I guess I think about Bobby Marshall so much because I don't see him very often. Bobby is really busy. And besides, he's terrified that someone from one of his teams might find out what's going on. Or his parents. I'm scared as well, but not like Bobby. He says he has an image to protect.

And me? Well, I also have an image to protect, though I guess my image is different from Bobby's. A nerd who likes words and speaks a foreign language at home. So if we add being gay to those things I guess it's just another weird thing about me. Maybe not even so weird when you consider the other things. I can hear someone say, "So, RV is gay. Big deal. He likes reading books like *Cancer Ward* or *Crime and Punishment* instead of listening to music or playing ball. Now that's weird!"

Bobby and I are really careful not to act too friendly at school. It does get me upset sometimes because he acts cold, and I'm afraid he's mad at me. We never leave school together or spend too much time together outside either. We don't hang out in the woods or even at Joe's Pizza together much. I miss that.

"What's wrong with having a pizza together at Joe's?" I asked him the other day while we were sitting in his room doing some homework together.

"I'm just nervous about it," Bobby said.

"But people don't know about me, either," I said. "It's not like I act like femme-y or anything."

"No," Bobby answered. But he looked a little guilty.

"What?" I asked. I could tell he was thinking about something he wasn't sure if he should tell me.

"What?" I repeated.

"Well," Bobby said finally. "The other day I heard some people talking about Mr. Aniso. And they mentioned that you had gone to visit him."

"They did?"

"They didn't say it was bad or anything. But they did notice."

"Who was it?"

"Some other students. I don't know them. But I heard them talking when I was passing one of the classrooms, and they were coming out."

That shouldn't be a big deal, I told myself, but I still had images of Duffy and Doyle pushing me against the lockers and asking me why I visited Mr. Aniso so often.

"Hey, RV. I'm sorry. I didn't mean to make you nervous," Bobby said. "I just wanted to show you how people do notice things. That's reality."

I turned to Bobby. "Bobby, do you feel bad about... About being friends with me?"

"No, not at all. I told you, I like you."

"But...?"

"But, well, I told you there's reality."

"Do you feel bad about the whole gay thing?"

"No, but... Well, I do think about it. A lot." He made a face. "I sometimes do wonder if it's right or wrong."

I didn't know what to say to that. He continued. "I'm sorry. When I think about a man and a woman having sex, it seems natural where their body parts go."

"You mean the penis in the vagina?"

Bobby nodded. "But two guys and two penises? Or what about two women and two vaginas...?" He didn't seem to know how to finish the sentence.

"I know what you mean," I said. "I think about that too. Doesn't seem natural at first." A thought came to me. "But then what is natural?"

"What do you mean?" Bobby asked.

"Well, like your mouth. Is it made for eating or kissing?"

"Good point," Bobby said. He seemed deep in thought. "It gets complicated if you really think about it."

I agreed. "I know. And I keep wondering why some people are gay while others are not. Like Tim, Carole's new boyfriend. He's a nerd like me, but as far as I can tell, he's not gay."

"Hey. Being a nerd has nothing to do with being gay," Bobby reminded me.

"No, I guess not." I agreed. "There I go stereotyping again."

"Yeah, macho jocks are gay too," Bobby said, giving me a playful punch. "Real guys are gay too."

"Oh, now who's stereotyping?" I said. "So I'm not a real guy?"

"Okay, got me there," Bobby laughed. "Guilty as charged. What is a real guy anyway?"

"Yeah, what is a real guy?"

"I'll show you." Bobby jumped up and wrestled me to the bed. "A real guy can take you in a wrestling match!" he said, pinning my arms to the bed.

"And I can spell Renaissance!" I had to say something to defend my honor. "And you're glad I can, aren't you?"

Bobby laughed. "I sure am! I'm thrilled real men can spell Renaissance!"

We wrestled some more, and of course I was no match for Bobby. He had me pinned down against the bed again pretty quickly.

Then he rolled off me and we were lying side by side, looking up at the ceiling.

"RV. Do you believe in God?" Bobby asked after a while.

"I'm not sure," I answered. "Sometimes yes, sometimes no. Why?"

"Just wondering. I guess I feel the same way. My parents are religious, and they raised me to think the world is a certain way. Right or wrong. Black or white. But I'm learning it's more complicated than that."

I nodded. "Yeah." I told him about my conversations with Mr. Aniso. "He wanted to be a priest. He believes in God, but he's not dogmatic about it." I thought for a second. "He makes me feel better about God," I said, turning to Bobby. "You might want to talk to him too."

"Yeah, maybe," Bobby said, but he didn't sound convinced.

"What's the matter?" I asked. "You really don't want to be seen with him, do you?"

"No, I guess not."

"You want to protect your image?"

Bobby turned to me. "I know it sounds terrible, RV, but it's more than that. I know Mr. Aniso is your friend. But that's your world, RV. I'm not in your world."

I didn't say anything, not sure what he was getting at.

"The thing is," he said, turning away, trying to explain himself. "I feel like I'm in a lot of worlds. Yes, a part of me is in your world. But then a part of me is in the football world, a part of me is in the black world, whatever that means. And a part of me is in my parents' world. Even though I get mad at them sometimes, especially my Dad, I still like being popular and making them proud of me." He turned back to me. "Does that make sense?"

"Yes, sure. I feel like I'm in different parts of the world too," I said. "Just different parts from you. Well, some different, some the same."

"Yeah," Bobby agreed. "Different in some ways. The same in other ways."

Bobby leaned over and propped himself up on one elbow. "It's nice, isn't it? Having someone who's like you in some important ways."

I nodded.

"Is that why we like each other?" Bobby asked.

"I don't know. I guess so."

Bobby was staring at me in that intent way he has, his dark eyes big and unblinking.

And then I couldn't believe what happened next. He leaned over me and gave me a kiss. On the lips.

My eyes had been closed when he kissed me. I opened them, and saw him look away sheepishly. "I'm sorry," he said. "I just wanted to know how it feels."

"And how did it feel?"

"Okay. Good."

I wanted to ask him how it compared to kissing Cynthia Hoevermeyer, but didn't dare.

Bobby lay back down on the bed and let out a strange little laugh. "Oh, RV," he said. "I'm so confused."

"Join the club," I said. And I can't believe what I did next. I leaned over and kissed him on the lips.

He looked a little surprised, but then he grabbed me, holding onto me tightly, and kissed me again. And then we both fell onto the bed, laughing.

"I can't believe we just did this," Bobby said.

"Neither can I."

We laughed some more. Then Bobby took my hand in his. "Actually, I've wanted to do it for a long time, RV. I was just afraid."

"Afraid? Of me?"

"Yeah. Or maybe me. I don't know. I told you I was confused."

We lay there for a long time, holding hands and looking up at the ceiling. We talked about a lot of things, including whether we could tell anyone about what was going on between us. But Bobby was adamant about that. He made me promise again not to say anything about it to anybody.

"Even Mr. Aniso?" I asked.

"Even Mr. Aniso."

"Okay," I promised, though I knew it wouldn't be easy. But a promise was a promise, right? I still had a zillion questions, and I could tell Bobby did too. But then I remembered again what Mr. Aniso said. That it's okay to have questions. And asking them is the first step in figuring things out in life. If that's true, then I guess Bobby and I are on our way.

*

I knew it was bad the minute I walked into the kitchen for dinner. Mom looked very upset, not saying anything, just staring down at the food on the table. I couldn't tell exactly, but her eyes were red, as if she'd been crying. Mom, crying? She never cried. This was bad.

Dad looked very upset too. He wasn't saying either, but from the expression on his face he actually appeared to feel sorry for Mom. Ray was there, too, doing his usual bit to ignore everyone as best he could.

I sat down quietly, after mumbling an excuse about being late. Mom glanced at me and told me to begin eating.

We started putting the food on our plates. I tried to eat but could hardly manage a bite, wondering what was going on. Finally Dad looked up from his food and said Mom had some bad news. About her jewelry business.

Oh-oh. Dad went back to eating, waiting for her tell us what happened. But Mom wasn't talking.

"So what happened to the frickin' business?" It was Ray. I guess he couldn't stand the silence either.

I expected Ray to get a reprimand for swearing, but Mom and Dad were too upset to notice. Dad turned to him and explained that the owner of the jewelry store had disappeared.

Ray's eyes opened wide. "And with him the money she gave him for rent?"

"*Taip,*" Dad said. "Yes." And he added that besides the $2,500, he made off with some of the jewelry.

So Mom had been taken in by a scam artist. Or an unscrupulous businessman.

This was almost worse than seeing Mom and Dad arguing. When she's upset, she gets angry too. And she stands up to Dad, no matter how frightening he looks. So I know she hasn't given up. That she's fighting for herself.

But now she looked like she couldn't lift a finger to help herself. "Mom, I'm sure you'll figure something out," I said, trying to think of something, anything, to make her feel better. "Carole and I can help you with your jewelry website so you can sell more. And I'm sure we'll come up with other ideas too."

Mom nodded, but she didn't look like she believed me. She suddenly got up, put her napkin down, and left the room without saying anything.

I glanced over at Dad. He gave me Ray and me an angry look.

"*Tai va, tau America.* So that's America for you." He repeated it. "*Tai va, tau America.*"

Ray, who had been watching this without saying a word, moved his chair away from the table, ready to run. I told myself to do the same thing. But neither of us moved.

Dad became silent. He wasn't looking at us, just staring at the table and breathing heavily. The breathing became heavier. Then he made a high-pitched sound, and his whole body started shaking. Then he started to cry.

This wasn't regular crying though. This was sobbing. Deep and hollow crying, as if Dad was trying to get some air from deep down in his chest, but he could never get enough. He would suck in some air, and then let out some sobs, while his whole body shook. And then he did the same thing again. And again.

Neither Ray nor I moved an inch. Dad crying? It was hard enough to see him angry. But to see Dad lose it like that? I don't think either of us knew what to do.

Finally, one of us made a move, and then we both left the table without saying anything to one another. I went to my room, and Ray went to his, leaving Dad sitting at the table, still crying.

*

I've been trying to write this all down, trying to drown out Dad's sobbing, which I can still hear from my room. But I'm doing it to drown out my own thoughts too.

I've been wondering what's going to happen now. Will Mom be able to make back that money? Will Dad do something desperate since he's always so worried about money? And if he does, will Mom start talking about a divorce again? Maybe now Dad will want one. I've been wondering about other things, too, things I'm afraid to think about too much.

I've been complaining a lot about my family. But now I'm afraid it's going to break apart. As bad as it can be, do I really want it to disappear? Maybe Dad is right in a weird way. Maybe family is everything. Could things be even worse without it?

*

"Hi."

"Oh, hi, Carole."

"How are things?"

"They're okay. How are things with you?"

"Okay."

I was having a pizza at you-know-where today, which is about the only place that makes me feel good when my family gets to me. And who showed up but Carole. Alone. Without Tim.

She stood there and I sat there without saying anything. "Can I...can I sit down?" she asked.

"Sure."

We still didn't say anything, and kept on looking at each other. "Where's Tim?" I asked, just to say something, though I don't think I really wanted to know the answer.

"He's gone shopping with his parents."

"Oh."

We sat there quietly for a bit. Carole finally broke the silence. "RV, are you mad at me?" she wanted to know.

"Why should I be mad?"

"I don't know. I was just wondering. I haven't heard from you..."

"I guess I just didn't want to bother you. I figured you were busy with Tim."

"Yeah, but my being with Tim doesn't mean we can't see each other or even talk."

"True." I could see Carole didn't like my answer. "But you could have called too," I told her.

"Yes," she agreed. "But...but I got the feeling you didn't want to hear from me... And I think you've been avoiding me at school."

"Why should I do that?" I asked. "We broke up, and that's done." Why was I lying? I still was a little mad at Carole. She did dump me, after all. What a great word. Like throwing something in the garbage. Is that what people are to each other after they've broken up? Garbage?

Carole wouldn't let it go though. "I can see you're still upset at me," she said. "I'm sorry. I miss you, and I wish we could be friends."

Why am I such a sucker when people say I'm sorry? Or when they look at me with pleading eyes like scared children? It must be something in my genes, along with all those other wonderful qualities my genes gave me.

"I guess I was a little upset," I told Carole. "I didn't know what I'd done wrong."

"You didn't do anything wrong!" Carole said. "Well, except for the fact I thought you were losing interest. And Tim was there."

"You could have said something."

"Yes, you're right. I said I'm sorry."

"It's okay."

"I hope it will be some day. I really do miss you."

We sat there quietly again. "Aren't you going to get any pizza?" I asked, realizing Carole was just sitting there, not eating anything.

"Oh, yeah. That is why I came here, isn't it?" she said, getting up out of her seat.

She went and got a slice of pizza. "So how's everything—really?" she asked when she came back.

"Well, I wonder if my parents are going to separate like yours," I said, and then I told her what happened to Mom. "It was awful."

"Wow," she said. "Two thousand five hundred dollars. Plus some jewelry. That really sucks!"

"Yeah," I said, not feeling any better.

"It's sad how quickly families can fall apart," Carole was saying. "Everybody is together, sharing their whole lives and then poof! They're gone." She grew wistful, getting a faraway look in her eyes. "I do miss my father. Even if he wasn't there a lot, he was still there sometimes. I guess I didn't appreciate it at the time."

We talked some more about our families. I was reminded how much Carole and I had to share. I did miss her. I missed her a lot.

"So are you seeing anyone?" she wanted to know.

I shook my head. Another lie. Lies were starting to come too easily to me.

"Are you sure?"

I nodded.

"Then why are you blushing?"

"I'm not blushing."

"Yes, you are."

Carole was giggling now. The giggle I knew so well.

"Come on, tell me. What's going on?"

"Nothing." How could I say anything to Carole. I had promised Bobby. I didn't have to mention him by name, but still.

"Okay, be that way." Carole looked upset.

I felt bad, but I just couldn't say anything.

We talked about other things as Carole finished her pizza. I reminded Carole about our computer business. "Or has Tim taken my place there too?" I almost said, but luckily stayed quiet. She told me she and Tim hadn't been giving it as much attention as it needed, and they needed me back to help push things along again.

We left Joe's Pizza after Carole was done and promised to call each other before going our separate ways.

"And I still want to know who you're going out with!" Carole called after me.

"Nobody!" I called back.

*

I'm glad I ran into Carole today, and I'm glad we talked and promised to call each other. But I'm not glad I said I was going out with nobody. Is Bobby a nobody to me?

Chapter Twenty

Nirvana

I did it! I made it through the first year of Latin school! Whew!

There was a ceremony to celebrate the end of the year. Parents were invited, and Mom and Dad came too. It's been a few weeks since that horrible dinner when Mom lost the money, but no one has said any more about divorce or splitting up. Not that Mom and Dad are hunky-dory or anything. Mom is working harder than ever trying to make back the money she lost, so she doesn't have time for much else. Dad doesn't say much, but at least he has stopped sniping—his way of being supportive, I suppose.

And they're talking. Talking! It's only about simple, everyday things, but hey, I'll take it. In our family that's pretty much nirvana. (I learned about nirvana from a book I read. It means heaven, sort of, but also how you'd want life to be if life was perfect. Which it never is. Which means you're always stressed trying to get to nirvana until you learn you can't, not in this life. So you just go with the flow, doing the best you can. I'm learning. I'm learning.)

I'm glad Mom, Dad, and Ray got it together to go with me to the ceremony. It was great. There were speeches by the headmaster and congratulations and awards. Bobby won a sports award. I applauded a lot when his name was called. His parents were there, too, and I saw them applauding and looking very proud. I know he saw me applaud for him, because he gave me a tiny smile when he walked by me going back to his seat. Do I wish the smile was bigger? Sure. But that's okay. I'm almost as nervous about us as he is. And besides, I know we're going to see each other over the summer. So today I could deal with pretending we're not close or anything. It bothers me a little bit, but like I said, I'm learning that life isn't nirvana in a lot of ways.

I was shocked when my name was called for an award. For getting all As and Bs and for perfect attendance. A couple of kids got the award, so at least I didn't have to go up there alone. I can just see Whalen putting it on Facebook and calling it the "RV the Angel" award.

But Mom and Dad seemed really happy when I walked back to my seat, so I guess it's worth it, no matter what it's called. Mom and Dad have been unhappy for so much of this year, it's nice to see them smile, really smile. It's a little scary that it's up to me to make them smile, but if it works I'm glad.

I'm learning other kids don't have perfect families either. Like Carole with her parents who are separated. Or even kids whose families appear perfect from the outside, like Bobby's. But he still needs to prove himself to his Dad. So a lot of us kids are in this pressure cooker together, aren't we?

We thought we were at the end of the ceremony when the headmaster came back on stage and said he had a surprise. An award to present. A special award from the Board of Trustees of the school. "To a teacher exemplifying many years of excellence," the headmaster said. "But most important, we want to welcome him back after many months." He talked about the teacher's courage in dealing with difficult circumstances, violence, and his continued commitment to the school. And then he said his name, "Gary Aniso."

The auditorium went wild as Mr. Aniso appeared on stage. He was walking with a cane, slowly, but he was walking. I was probably the first one out of my seat, cheering and applauding and yelling his name. I didn't care who saw me or who heard me. I wanted to give Mr. Aniso my own award for so many things. But I was glad, too, that most people were cheering and applauding. Even Duffy and Doyle, who I saw sitting off in the distance. Were they really happy for Mr. Aniso? Or were they pretending? At the moment, it didn't matter. Everyone seemed happy for him. And it was like a piece of me was up there with him, enjoying the applause.

Mr. Aniso spoke a little bit when the applause finally died down. His voice still sounded weak, and everyone had to listen really carefully to his words. But we were so glad when he said he was thrilled to be back and that he was looking forward to teaching again next fall.

And then he said, "And thank you for all your support and your cards and visits. It's because of you that I'm back." I don't know. Maybe it's my imagination, but I honestly think he was looking at me when he thanked us for the visits. How he could even tell where I was sitting is anyone's guess, but if he was really looking at me, I'm glad.

*

I want to write more about the ceremony, which was this afternoon, but I've spent the last hour texting and talking to my friends. We were all congratulating each other, and making plans for the summer. Bobby texted me, and he sounded happy. We're going to see each other tomorrow. I'm glad he's keeping his promise of seeing me so soon. He doesn't get much of a break before he has to start practice again for one team or another. I guess jocks have their work cut out for them too.

I had to do one thing though. I called Carole up and asked her if she had any time to see me. Alone. I told her I wanted to talk to her. I didn't see her at the ceremony and felt bad about it. She told me she was there and felt bad about not seeing me either. We're going to get together tonight. This will be interesting.

*

Life might not be nirvana, but sometimes it comes close. Like tonight, with Carole.

We decided not to go to Joe's Pizza, but to meet outside and take a walk. It's nice and warm out, and the coming of summer always fills me with happy thoughts. We met near Carole's house.

"Hi."

"Hi."

I couldn't believe it. There we were, both looking at each other nervously. I guess we both realized we had some catching up to do.

"I hope Tim doesn't mind that I asked you to come alone," I said.

Carole shook her head. "No. Tim's not the jealous type."

"Good. Thanks for coming out to see me," I said, as we started to walk down the street. "I missed you at the ceremony."

"Yeah, sorry. I was with Mom and Dad and their friends."

"Your Dad came too?"

Carole nodded. "Yeah, that was a nice surprise. He said he wanted to do it for me, but Mom seemed happy about it."

"Maybe they'll get back together again."

"I don't know about that," Carole said. "Maybe. I'm just happy for today. I don't want to expect too much."

It was my turn to nod. "I know what you mean." We talked about nirvana, and how we all want it but can't get it.

"And how are your folks?" she asked.

I told her about Mom working hard to pay the money back, but that there was no talk about divorce now. "I guess I'm like you," I said. "I'm just happy for today."

Carole suddenly flung her arms around me and gave me a big hug. "Oh, RV, I've missed you. We have such good talks," she said. Then she got that sparkly little look in her eyes. "You know, sometimes talks are better than making out."

I couldn't help laughing. "You mean Tim isn't as good a talker as I was?" I couldn't help saying.

"Oh, RV. Please don't be jealous of Tim. He's a little intense but a good guy, but... But I want to be friends with you too. Can't that be possible? I miss you."

"No. You're right," I said. "If Tim likes you, he has to be a good guy."

Carole was right. She and I do have good talks. There was so much I wanted to tell her. That's why I had called her. But now we were walking, and feeling close, I couldn't start talking. I still don't know why the most important things in life are the hardest to talk about.

It was slowly getting dark, and lights were coming on in the houses we passed by. The lights looked soft and inviting, like they wanted to embrace us and protect us from the dark. I was thinking about the ceremony again and told Carole how great it was to see Mr. Aniso at school again.

"Yes!" she exclaimed. "I wish I had him for a teacher. He seems like a great guy."

I nodded. "I got to know him better during my visits to the hospital."

"Oh? I didn't know you saw him at the hospital."

"Yeah. I—I guess I didn't tell you. I went a couple of times."

"I didn't know you were that close," Carole said. She looked like she was thinking about something she wanted to say but didn't know how.

"Yeah, you see, I needed to go see him," I told her. "Well, I didn't need to. But I wanted to. Because... Because I thought he could teach me a lot of things." I looked at Carole and swallowed—hard, a few times. "I thought he could teach me things about... About being gay."

"About being gay?"

"Yes."

She looked at me, but didn't say anything. I knew I had to say it.

"Because I might be."

"Gay? You?"

"Yes."

"Yes!" Carole exclaimed again and threw her arms around me. "Oh, RV. I'm so glad!"

"You are?"

"Well, yeah," Carole said. "I could tell for a long time that something was going on between us, something we couldn't talk about. And for a long time I thought it was something I did. Or that you didn't like me. But it's just that you're gay!"

"I said I might be gay."

"Whatever." Carole didn't seem interested in any fine points about being gay.

"So you don't mind?"

"Mind? I'm thrilled! So we really can be friends again, right?" Carole raised her arms and twirled around like she was about to start dancing. I was afraid she'd start to get the attention of the people in the houses. Maybe I should have picked another place to tell her.

Carole must have seen that I looked nervous, so she came up to me and threw her arms around me again. "Don't worry. I won't tell anyone about it," she said more quietly. "Not that it should be a secret, but it's up to you to tell people."

She turned to me. "Are you going to say anything to your parents?"

I shook my head and shrugged. "I don't know." I told her about feeling like different people sitting at the dinner table with Mom and Dad. "I want to tell them, but I can't. Not now anyway. They've got so many other crazy things going on." I told her about Dad crying and more details about Mom losing the money. "I just can't tell them. Not now. Maybe someday."

We walked on quietly. I must have started thinking about my family again because when I glanced up Carole was looking at me intently.

"RV. I'm so glad you told me," she said quietly. "It means a lot to me."

"Oh, Carole. I'm so glad we're friends," I said, giving her giving her an even bigger hug than she gave me. "It's good to have friends you can trust."

"That's for sure," Carole said. "It doesn't happen often in life." Then she turned to me. "Do you have... Are you seeing anyone?"

I wanted to tell her about Bobby, but I remembered my promise to him. "No," I said. "Nobody in particular."

There was that word again. Bobby wasn't nobody. But I had promised not to say anything about him to anyone. And here was another word. Trust. Trust between friends, which Carole and I just finished talking about. So was I breaking that trust with Carole? Life was too complicated sometimes.

Carole grew quiet again, probably sensing all these thoughts flying around in my head.

But then she leaned over and whispered in my ear. "Hey, RV. Let's go to the woods. I still think of it as our special place."

"You sure?" I asked. I didn't want to tell her I'd been there with Bobby. And I was sure she'd been there with Tim.

But Carole insisted. "I like it there. Let's not think about anything else. We just know it makes us feel good, right?"

So we made our way over there. The moon was shining really brightly, and it was easy to find a nice dry spot by the stream.

We sat down and hugged each other. Carole was right. I felt good sitting there too. The moon was almost full, and it illuminated the trees around us and the hills in the distance. *Life might not be nirvana, but it's still full of promise*, I told myself.

"What are you thinking?" whispered Carole.

"Oh, that I'm glad to have a friend like you to share things with. Life might not be nirvana, but it's still full of promise," I repeated out loud.

Carole laughed. "Wow! You're a poet, RV," she said. Then she snuggled closer to me. "Some guy is going to be lucky to have you."

I'm glad it was too dark for her to see me blush. I wondered if I'd be talking to her about Bobby someday.

We sat there watching the moon for a long time. What a day. The ceremony at school and having Mr. Aniso back. Seeing Bobby tomorrow. And sitting here with Carole under a bright moon. For a nerdy kid I'm not doing so bad, am I?

About the Author

Andy V. Roamer grew up in the Boston area and moved to New York City after college. He worked in book publishing for many years, starting out in the children's and YA books division and then wearing many other hats. This is his first novel about RV, the teenage son of immigrants from Lithuania in Eastern Europe, as RV tries to negotiate his demanding high school, his budding sexuality, and new relationships. He has written an adult novel, *Confessions of a Gay Curmudgeon*, under the pen name Andy V. Ambrose. To relax, Andy loves to ride his bike, read, watch foreign and independent movies, and travel.

Email: andyvroamer@gmail.com

Facebook: www.facebook.com/andyvroamer

Website: www.andyvroamer.com

Coming Soon from Andy V. Roamer

Why Can't Summer Be Like Pizza?
The Pizza Chronicles Book 2

I used to love summer. The long, languid days. No school. No homework. Sleeping late. Going to the beach. Staying out later in the evenings and watching the sun set over the hills into the darkening glow of the horizon.

Wow. Am I starting to sound like a poet or just a pretentious a-hole? What's wrong with the paragraph I just wrote? There are no pretentious words in it, are there? Well, maybe "languid" is. I like "languid." I don't know where I picked it up, but I think it perfectly describes everything about summer. Where everything is a little more s-l-l-o-o-w-w-w and easygoing. Where life seems good, and there's no homework. Yup, I'll stick with languid. Hey, there has to be a benefit to liking words the way I do. I'm not only a nerd, but a poetic nerd.

Ha ha ha. Maybe it has something to do with being bilingual. I never used to think about it much before, but I guess I am officially bilingual. Talking Lithuanian at home. English in the outside world. Just kind of always accepted it, didn't I? But I wonder what speaking two languages does to someone. Kind of like being split into two people. My Lith life and my English life. Are there really two people inside me? Scary thought. One of me is bad enough.

Luckily, Bobby Marshall doesn't seem to be bothered by it, so why should I be?

Ahh, Bobby Marshall. I still can't believe we're friends. Or should I say "special friends?" I'm still afraid to even think about it. Me, RV Aleksandravičius—nerd extraordinaire, spawn of Lithuanian immigrants, word lover, nervous worrywuss, possible gay person—friends with one of the biggest jocks in school. The world truly is an amazing place.

But, as I was saying, I *used to* love summer. That was before I had to work. This summer I'll be toiling away like the rest of humanity. And I'm not just talking about working with the computer fix-it company I started last year with Carole. The business has been kind of rocky lately. I'll blame it on the bad economy since everyone always blames everything on a bad economy.

No, I'm working at my first real job. I turned fifteen last week. I used to love my birthdays. The end of school. The start of summer. But not anymore. Dad has a friend at work, Mr. Timmons, whose brother, Ed, owns a garage and gas station. Dad was talking to him and lo and behold (another pretentious choice of words?), Mr. Timmons told him Ed was looking for someone to help with chores around the place. Since I'm not sixteen yet, I'm not supposed to work in the garage itself. But I can dispense gas, and I work around the store Ed has attached to the garage. Nothing heavy duty, Mr. Timmons said. Ed just needs someone fifteen to twenty hours a week helping in the store and cleaning around the place. A great way to earn a little pocket money.

Also Available from NineStar Press

Connect with NineStar Press

www.ninestarpress.com

www.facebook.com/ninestarpress

www.facebook.com/groups/NineStarNiche

www.twitter.com/ninestarpress

www.tumblr.com/blog/ninestarpress

www.ingramcontent.com/pod-product-compliance
Lightning Source LLC
Chambersburg PA
CBHW050523190726
48284CB00003B/927